It was just like in a ghost tov
there wouldn't be a child's
garden fence, nor a skippi
pavement.

What was more, lights were shining from several houses, so there were people living here after all.

People ... Tony studied the group of vampires and a shudder ran down his spine. He would have preferred a less deserted neighbourhood – just in case of an emergency!

Follow the spooky adventures of Tony and his vampire friends in this new series of *The Little Vampire* books:

Angela Sommer-Bodenburg

the little Vampire

LEARNS TO BE BRAVE

Translated by Sarah Gibson

Illustrated by Anthony Lewis

SIMON & SCHUSTER
YOUNG BOOKS

Text copyright © 1990 C. Bertelsmann Verlag GmbH, Munich
Illustrations copyright © 1993 Anthony Lewis

First published in Germany in 1990 by C. Bertelsmann Verlag GmbH

First published in Great Britain in 1993
by Simon & Schuster Young Books
Campus 400
Maylands Avenue
Hemel Hempstead
Herts HP2 7EZ

Set in 12pt Goudy Old Style by
Derek Doyle & Associates, Mold, Clwyd
Printed and bound by the
Guernsey Press Co Ltd, Channel Islands

British Library Cataloguing in Publication Data available

ISBN 0 7500 1371 0
ISBN 0 7500 1372 9 (pb)

Contents

The Story So Far...

Tony's best friends are Rudolph and Anna Sackville-Bagg, who are both vampires! They live with their creepy Aunt Dorothy and their unpredictable teenage brother, Greg, in the family vault in the cemetery.

Tony's parents don't believe in vampires, and they have become so worried about Tony's obsession with them that they are sending him to a psychologist, Mr Crustscrubber. But Tony has discovered that Mr Crustscrubber has a *vampire* as one of his patients – the mysterious Igno von Rant – on whom the psychologist is trying out his new course of treatment for people who are scared of sunlight.

Rudolph, the Little Vampire, has persuaded Tony to let him start Mr Crustscrubber's "desensitisation" treatment. And Anna, who is in love with Tony, also wants to learn how to see in daylight, so that she can spend much more time with Tony . . .

This book is for Burghardt,
who thinks the Sommer-Bodenburg house is the bees'
knees – as well as everything that creeps and crawls,
whether it wears a vampire cloak or not!

In Tip-Top Form – for Bed!

One Sunday morning, Tony was woken by some strange hopping sounds. Prising open his eyes, he found his father going through his early morning exercises at the foot of the bed.

He wasn't wearing pyjamas or a dressing-gown, but a tracksuit and trainers, which was most unusual for a Sunday morning.

Tony felt he must still be in the middle of a dream – or rather, a nightmare . . .

He shut his eyes, then opened them again, blinking cautiously. But his father was still there.

"Why have you woken me up so early?" he grumbled.

"Early?" His father laughed. "It's nearly eleven o'clock! Mum and I have just decided that this Sunday we're going to join a proper Keep Fit club in the park!"

"We?" asked Tony suspiciously. It was slowly dawning on him just why his father was jumping about by his bed. "You mean me too?"

"Of course!" replied Dad. "You need to get into shape more than anyone!"

"Oh, no!" groaned Tony, pulling his bedclothes up to his nose.

"Oh, yes!" said Dad. "You don't seem particularly lively this morning!" And with a confidential wink, he went on, "Watching TV late last night, were you? What was on? *Dracula abandons the tomb* or *Frankenstein's Widow?*"

1

"Not likely!" said Tony.

"Well, what about the late-night movie?" joked Dad. "Wasn't that up your street?"

"For a start, you know perfectly well I'm not allowed to watch the late-night movie," answered Tony. "And secondly, I was already asleep by that time!"

It was true. The previous evening Tony and the Little Vampire had visited the psychologist, Mr Crustscrubber, at his practice, and the Little Vampire had found out about the treatment for curing people of phobias. He had flown away afterwards, and Tony had had to fly home all by himself. He had arrived back in his room pretty exhausted, and had gone straight to bed.

"Oh, really?" said Dad, giving him a conspiratorial wink. Tony looked at him haughtily and said nothing.

"Are you both ready?" Mum now appeared in the room, dressed in a dark blue tracksuit.

"What! Still in bed Tony?" she exclaimed.

"Our son isn't in tip-top form today," joked Dad. "At least, only in tip-top form for bed!"

"Ha, ha!" said Tony, without batting an eyelid. Slowly he pushed back the bedclothes.

"Who knows how late he's had his light on!" said his mother thoughtfully.

Tony grinned. "Yes, who knows . . . "

But his mother went on briskly, "Hurry up and get dressed." Then she left the room.

"See you in a minute, old sport!" remarked Dad, following her out.

I Forgot It!

When his parents had gone, Tony suddenly remembered something dreadful! He had left his bag behind at Mr Crustscrubber's the evening before – the bag containing his new yellow tracksuit. Wouldn't it be wiser to stay in bed under the circumstances? he wondered. He could always say he had a headache. But then Mum would come fussing round with an ice pack and some medicine.

No, there was nothing else for it. He would have to get up. Feeling uneasy, he pulled on his jeans and green hooded pullover. As he did so, he racked his brains for an excuse as to why he wasn't wearing his new tracksuit; it would have to be a good one to convince Mum!

"Tony?" It was his mother's voice again, and there she was, standing in the doorway.

Just as Tony had guessed, she exclaimed with annoyance at the sight of him. "You're wearing your old clothes!"

"Mmm, yes," said Tony.

"But it's Sunday!"

Tony tried to keep his expression normal.

"I didn't know you had to dress up on a Sunday in this house!"

"You don't have to dress up!" she retorted irritably. "But if I buy you a new tracksuit – and that yellow one was particularly expensive, as you know! – then I expect you to wear it!"

"I, er . . . " At first, Tony thought of saying he'd put on his old clothes so that his new tracksuit wouldn't wear out so quickly. But he suspected that this wouldn't wash with Mum, so he admitted, "I forgot it."

"Forgot it? You forgot it?" Mum gasped. "Where?"

Tony hesitated. He couldn't really say "At Ollie's house", because then she would insist that he go and fetch it immediately. What if he said, "With Rudolph Sackville-Bagg?" His parents thought the Little Vampire and his sister Anna had moved to another town and vanished out of Tony's life. This might be just the moment to explain that Rudolph and Anna had come back again . . .

He quickly dismissed this idea too. However, the thought of the Little Vampire had given him an idea.

"I left the tracksuit at Geoff 's house!" he said. And that was actually the truth!

"Geoff?" Tony's mother looked as though she didn't believe him. "That's the first time I've heard that name!"

"Could be," said Tony, laughing secretly to himself. Geoff was Mr Crustscrubber's first name. So far, Tony's mother had probably only ever *read* the psychologist's Christian name – on the brass plate by the surgery door!

"Is he a new boy in your class?"

"A new boy?" drawled Tony. He remembered a dream he had had once, that he was about to become enrolled as a "new boy" in the Sackville-Bagg family . . .

"More like a new blood-brother!"

"OK, OK! You can joke about it!" Tony's mother sounded angry now. "But I can tell you one thing: whatever sort of brother this Geoff turns out to be, your tracksuit must be back here in your cupboard by tomorrow evening!"

With these words, she swept out of the room.

"Shall I stay at home then?" called Tony hopefully after her. "I mean, because it's Sunday and I've only got my old things?"

"Of course not!" Mum yelled back.

"What about other people?" Tony had one more try. "What will they think of us, if I'm going around in scruffy old clothes on a Sunday? Don't you mind?"

"Of course I mind!" she snapped. "You can always keep your distance. Stand a metre away from us!"

"Fine by me!" growled Tony. Just to annoy her, he added, "A whole kilometre away, as far as I'm concerned!"

But this time she didn't reply and so Tony trotted crossly out into the hall.

However, contrary to all his expectations, it turned out to be a really nice Sunday. They had hot chocolate and Danish pastries in the café in the park – "As a treat because it's Sunday," as Mum put it. And when Tony had run twice round the paddling pool, he even got an ice-cream with a chocolate flake stuck in it as a reward!

"I only hope your stomach can stand all these sweet things!" Mum couldn't resist saying.

"Don't worry!" Tony grinned. "It's in tip-top condition!"

But his muscles weren't in such a good condition he realized the next morning as soon as he got out of bed. They felt even worse that afternoon, when he got on his bike to ride round to "Geoff 's house" and pick up his tracksuit. The things he did for Mum!

"Where does Geoff live, by the way?" she had asked him as he set off.

"Oh, not far from here," he answered vaguely. Not far – that was a good one!

When Tony finally reached Mr Crustscrubber's house,

he felt well and truly exercised!

He dragged himself up the steps to the front door and rang the bell. Mrs Crustscrubber opened it and said in surprise: "Oh, it's you, Tony!"

"I left my bag here."

"All right, sit down for a moment in the waiting room."

"Sit down? Oh, yes please!"

Tony dropped into the deep, comfortable armchair by the window, and stretched out his legs. He was sitting like this when the door opened, and to his surprise, Mr Crustscrubber himself came into the room.

"Unfortunately I haven't got much time," said the psychologist apologetically. "I have a patient with me."

He gave Tony the bag.

"But before I go back, I'd just like to know what Rupert said!"

Encourage Him!

"Ru-Rupert?" stuttered Tony. He'd probably never get used to the false name the Little Vampire had given the psychologist.

"What he said about what?"

"About the trial session, of course! Surely Rupert told you what effect the treatment had on him!"

"Me? No!"

"Didn't he say anything at all about it?"

"No, because – he had to go," Tony replied hesitantly. He didn't like playing informer.

The psychologist looked disappointed. "So you can't tell me whether Rupert has decided to continue with the course or not?"

"No."

"Hmmm. It's very important that he should decide to go on with the course!" Mr Crustscrubber pulled at his moustache. "Particularly now, when I fear that Igno von Rant may have left me in the lurch!"

"What do you mean – left you in the lurch?" asked Tony, in alarm.

"Well, he's missed his appointment three times now!" answered Mr Crustscrubber.

"Three times?" Tony was shocked.

Mr Crustscrubber nodded. "Yes. And he didn't cancel beforehand either."

Tony gulped. Igno von Rant was the mysterious

patient Mr Crustscrubber was already treating for abnormally strong fears. It had seemed that the treatment was working well, for Igno von Rant (who Tony was convinced was a real vampire) had apparently gone a long way towards overcoming his fear of sunlight, or "sun phobia" as Mr Crustscrubber called it.

"Do you think something could have happened to him?" asked Tony in dismay. "I mean, if his sun phobia hasn't been properly cured, suppose he's gone out in the sunshine and got . . . cooked?"

"No, I don't think so," said Mr Crustscrubber firmly. "He had progressed so far with the treatment."

"But perhaps that *is* the reason!" he went on after a pause. "Perhaps Igno von Rant was satisfied with what he had achieved. The desensitivisation treatment is very strenuous, after all, and it demands great determination to stick at it —" Mr Crustscrubber broke off.

"I must go back to my patient. Just one more request, Tony: When you next see Rupert, do encourage him – encourage him as much as you can!" Before Tony could say anything else, Mr Crustscrubber had left the waiting room.

Tony stood up, his head swimming.

"Encourage him?" It might be wiser to warn the Little Vampire!

Bewildered, and with aching legs, Tony finally reached home again.

"We thought Geoff must have invited you to supper!" said Dad when he came in.

"Have I been away that long?" said Tony in surprise.

"Yes, you have!" said Mum, giving him a dark look. "We were beginning to think you'd decided to stay the night!"

Tony gave a weak smile. "Should I have?" he asked.

But he was too tired to get involved in an argument with his parents. Instead, he laid out the tracksuit on the middle of the kitchen table and disappeared off to his room, saying he had some maths homework to do.

Once in his room he went straight to bed, so that he would be a bit more refreshed when – as he earnestly hoped – the Little Vampire came and knocked on his window that night. He needed to talk to him urgently about Mr Crustscrubber and the latest worrying development in the story of Igno von Rant!

A Vampire's
Middle Name

But the Little Vampire didn't turn up that night nor the following one. Nor did Anna. Tony became more and more worried.

Saturday arrived and the evening when Rudolph had his second appointment with Mr Crustscrubber. At half past seven, Tony's parents left the flat. They had been invited over to friends.

Tony opened his window, sat down on his bed and picked up *"Werewolves – the Thirteen Best Stories"*. Soon he was absorbed in a brilliantly spooky story, and he never noticed the time pass, so when a figure landed on his windowsill and croaked "Hallo, Tony!" he nearly jumped out of his skin.

"Ha-hallo, Rudolph!" he stuttered, hastily pushing the book under his pillow.

The Little Vampire climbed down into the room and came over to the bed.

"Hey," I thought you'd have been ready ages ago!" he hissed, looking Tony over with glittering eyes. "But you haven't even got your cloak on yet!"

"I – I didn't know you'd come so early!" Tony excused himself.

"Early? Do you call this early?" The vampire gave his grating laugh, and clicked his strong, needle-sharp teeth together. "But you're right. Today I've been really quick, haven't I? Heh, heh!" With a slight shudder, Tony gazed at the vampire's lips, which looked full and deep red in the light of his bedside lamp. But at least he knew the Little Vampire had already eaten!

"Now I'm really greedy to get to old Mr Crustscrubber at long last!" the vampire went on.

"Greedy?" Tony repeated uneasily.

"Did I say 'greedy'?" The Little Vampire gave another of his laughs. "I meant, of course, that I can't wait. I'm really keen to get going with the treatment!"

"We . . . we must have a talk about that first!" said Tony.

"Talk about it?" said the vampire, not sounding at all enthusiastic. He seemed to be in rather a bad mood. It wasn't going to be the best time to discuss such serious problems with him, but Tony would just have to try!

"You know I told you about that vampire—" he began.

"Which vampire?" Rudolph interrupted.

"I was just going to explain! The vampire that's another patient of Mr Crustscrubber's – Igno von Rant. He's missed his appointment three times now, and didn't cancel once!"

"So what?" said the Little Vampire, shrugging his shoulders. "He's probably got his reasons – Mr Igno the Runt. And in any case, what's this buddy of yours got to do with me?"

"For a start, he's not my 'buddy'!" Tony said sharply. Thank goodness! he added to himself. "And secondly, something might have happened to him – something connected with the treatment!"

The Little Vampire pricked up his ears. "With the treatment?"

"Yes!" Tony cleared his throat, because he knew he was about to mention a delicate subject. "If Igno von Rant has stayed out in the sunlight too long, he might—"

"He might what?" demanded the vampire.

"He might have – got cooked!"

"Cooked?" repeated the vampire in a sepulchral voice. "You're only saying that because you're jealous!"

"What makes you think that?"

"You want to put me off the treatment because you're jealous of Olga!"

"Me? Of Olga?" Tony almost laughed.

"Course you are!" exclaimed the vampire. "You never liked Olga, and now that she wants to come all the way back from Vienna, to me, you're thinking up ways of keeping us apart!"

Tony shook his head. "No, I'm not!"

"Oh, yes, you are!" said the vampire. "You've never said one nice word about Olga! And why not?"

He looked penetratingly at Tony. Tony was wise enough not to reply that the trouble with Olga was, there was nothing nice you could say about her!

"Because you're annoyed that I . . . well, I have such affectionate feelings for Olga!" The Little Vampire answered his own question, obviously proud to demonstrate how shrewd he was!

Tony was afraid he would never get Rudolph to see sense when he was so blinded with love. So he tried reassurance. "I didn't say that to try to keep you two apart. I just wanted to warn you about Igno von Rant. But if you think I'm *against* you . . . "

"Not against *me*!" said the Little Vampire. "Against *Olga*!"

Tony gave a barely audible sigh. "All right, let's go then," he said.

"At last!" growled the vampire, as he climbed on to the windowsill and flew off into the night.

Tony took his vampire cloak out of the cupboard,

13

pulled it round his shoulders, switched off the light, and set off after the Little Vampire.

"Hurry up!" the vampire urged from outside. "I don't want to be late because of you!"

"Because of me indeed!" thought Tony grimly. He'd tried so hard to warn the Little Vampire of the trouble ahead, and all Rudolph could do was to blame *him*!

"Ingratitude is a vampire's middle name!" he said, but quietly so that the vampire wouldn't hear him.

Tummy Ache

They weren't late at all. As they landed behind the rose bushes in front of Mr Crustscrubber's house, the clock on the chemist's shop was just showing twenty past nine.

"We're ten minutes early, you see!" said Tony triumphantly.

"Huh! Well, you've got me to thank for that!" retorted the Little Vampire conceitedly. "I zoomed off at such a speed that you were drawn along with me – sucked along, perhaps I should say!"

"Oh, really?" said Tony scornfully.

"Yes, and it was also thanks to our cloaks – these original Sackville-Bagg cloaks!" the vampire went on. "In case you didn't know, these cloaks were made by my grandmother herself, Sabina the Sinister! She'd really blow a fuse if she knew that you – a human! – had been wearing her cloak!" he added with a giggle.

"*Her* cloak?" said Tony in surprise. "I thought it was Uncle Theodore's."

"It was," answered the Little Vampire. "But she made it. Back in Transylvania, before she started getting all those tummy aches."

"Tummy aches?" repeated Tony, not sure whether to feel sorry for her or disbelieve the story. "Is she ill?"

"She's suffering from a terrible illness!" declared the Little Vampire, in a miserable voice. "And I think I've

caught it off her. I feel so odd all of a sudden . . . " His face twisted and he pressed his hands to his tummy. As he did so, he looked up at the clock on the chemist's shop. The big hand was just on "6".

"Half past nine!" said Tony. "Come on, Mr Crustscrubber will be waiting for us. Or rather, for you!"

"Don't leave me!" cried the Little Vampire. "Not when I feel all funny!"

"It's probably excitement!" said Tony.

"Excitement?" said the vampire in a feeble voice.

"Yes," said Tony, suppressing a grin. "After all, Olga's coming back very soon . . . "

"Do you think that's why I feel like this?" asked the Little Vampire, a lovesick smile spreading across his face.

"I'm sure it is!" said Tony. As he said so, he glanced anxiously at the clock. It was now twenty-five to ten.

"Come on, Rudolph!" Tony moved determinedly towards the door. When he was sure the Little Vampire had followed him, he pressed Mr Crustscrubber's doorbell – two short rings, then two long rings, as they had arranged.

Heavy footsteps could be heard coming nearer, and then there was Mr Crustscrubber himself at the door. 'I was just thinking you weren't going to come any more!' he said.

Tony glanced at the vampire and replied with a grin, "We had a couple of problems with the flight."

"With the flight?" Mr Crustscrubber smirked. He obviously thought it was a joke. "I was worried that Rupert had decided not to continue with the treatment."

"No, no, I've decided I *will!*" Rudolph answered in his husky voice.

"I'm so pleased!" Mr Crustscrubber sighed deeply. "Come on in!"

Tony went in, and the Little Vampire followed hesitantly.

"What sort of problems did you have?" inquired the psychologist, as they climbed the steps to his consulting room.

"Well— " Tony glanced sideways at the vampire, and grinned. "These old vampire cloaks have got thousands of holes in them – they're not exactly aerodynamic. And Rud—, er, Rupert was a bit slow today."

"Me? Slow?" cried the Little Vampire indignantly.

Tony took no notice of this interruption. "You see, his health's under rather a strain at the moment."

"Huh!" snorted the vampire, stepping in front of Tony and brandishing a fist menacingly under his nose. "You'll be the one under a strain soon, traitor!"

"I can't believe it!" said Mr Crustscrubber. "You've hardly arrived, and you're already having a go at each other!"

"We?" snapped the Little Vampire. "It's Tony who's having a go!"

"So it's Tony who's beating the air with his fists, is it?" asked Mr Crustscrubber.

The Little Vampire let his arms fall to his sides and hissed, "You're just on his side!"

But the psychologist showed no reaction.

"I think it would be better if Tony stayed in the waiting room this time," he said.

For a second, the Little Vampire was speechless. Then he cried, "I won't be able to relax without Tony. If Tony isn't there, you can forget your treatment!"

"All right then," Mr Crustscrubber gave in. "Let's all go into the consulting room."

"And can Tony stay?" asked the Little Vampire, just to make completely sure.

"On condition that you're a bit more polite!" said Tony with a grin.

"Oh, I'll be super-polite!" growled the vampire.

Shadow Boxing

When they got to the psychologist's consulting room, the Little Vampire went straight over to the large, green leather armchair in which he had relaxed during the trial session. Sitting down, he went through a series of extraordinary arm movements, as though he were shadow boxing!

"Are these gestures meant to tell us something, Rupert?" asked Mr Crustscrubber. He was sitting on his swivel chair behind his large desk, which was strewn with books and papers as usual, and was watching the Little Vampire curiously.

"What do you mean, tell you something?" mumbled the vampire.

"What you're doing looks very mysterious!" remarked the psychologist.

"Mysterious?" repeated the Little Vampire. "I'm relaxing!"

"Oh, I see— " Mr Crustscrubber scratched his chin. He was obviously annoyed that he hadn't recognized Rudolph's "relaxation movements" for what they were!

Pulling himself together, he began to speak again in his calm, friendly psychologist's voice. "Well, it's wonderful that you've already started! It means we can continue with the exercises straight away, if that's all right with you!"

"Of course it's all right with me!" hissed the vampire.

"Can't you see how I am burning to start the treatment?"

"Burning?" Mr Crustscrubber cleared his throat. "Well, you're certainly a little less pale today than you were last time!"

Tony couldn't help grinning.

That's not surprising, when Rudolph's burning with love! he thought. But he didn't want to start any more arguments, so he kept the thought to himself.

He sat expectantly on the hard, wooden chair in front of Mr Crustscrubber's desk and listened as the psychologist began the exercises:

"Clench your right hand into a fist, Rupert, tight . . . feel the tension, that's right . . . And now let your fingers go slack, relax them . . . You're completely relaxed . . . "

The Little Vampire was concentrating harder today, and didn't seem to be as tense and worried either, Tony thought. Rudolph only interrupted the exercises once, because he said his arms were feeling "as heavy as lead coffins!" Apart from that, he followed the instructions without complaining, relaxing his arms, his neck and then his shoulders.

The strange silence which accompanied these exercises began to have an effect on Tony. He hardly dared breathe.

But when the Little Vampire was told to relax his face muscles, the atmosphere lightened. All of a sudden, Tony had the greatest difficulty not to laugh: it was so funny to see the way the Little Vampire puckered his forehead into a frown and made himself look like a sad little dachshund!

Then he was told to close his eyes, and Tony saw to his amazement that this time Rudolph's eyelids did not twitch at all. He glanced at Mr Crustscrubber to show his admiration.

The psychologist's calm, clear instructions seemed to have an almost hypnotic effect on the Little Vampire.

"Now you will count slowly backwards, beginning with five!" continued Mr Crustscrubber. "And then you will say: 'I feel well, I'm wide awake and very happy!' and you will open your eyes!"

In a hollow voice, the vampire began to count. "Five . . . four . . . three . . . two . . . one . . . I feel well, I'm wide awake and very happy—"

He opened his eyes and whistled softly through his teeth. "I really *am* wide awake, and I feel great!" he said, adding with a peal of throaty laughter, "Your treatment's almost as good as a blood transfusion! Ha, ha!"

Tony shuddered, but Mr Crustscrubber smiled and looked flattered. "I am very pleased that it has such a *positive* effect on you!" he said. "My other patient, Igno von Rant, always complained of headaches after the first session."

"Headaches?" said the vampire, tapping his forehead. "That's a foreign word to me." Then he added conceitedly, "It depends what sort of head you have!"

"Or how much wood there is in it!" added Tony. At once he could have kicked himself for saying such a stupid thing. But the Little Vampire didn't even look at Tony – it seemed as though the remark had escaped him.

The Sun Has Got His Hat On

"As far as I'm concerned, we could easily do a couple more exercises," declared the Little Vampire, turning to Mr Crustscrubber.

"I don't want you to tire yourself, Rupert," answered the psychologist.

"Oh— " said the vampire, "I'm used to my nerves being trampled on!"

"Really?" Mr Crustscrubber sounded concerned.

"Well, yes— " The Little Vampire grinned maliciously and nodded towards Tony. "If you've got a friend – er, I mean, if you've got someone like *him* around!"

For a minute Tony was tempted to say something unkind in return. But then he told himself that it was Rudolph's revenge for the remark about wooden heads, so he contented himself with scowling at the vampire.

"No, I really do think that's enough for one day!" declared Mr Crustscrubber.

He obviously felt that there was a new quarrel in the air. "Let's leave it till next Saturday, Rupert!"

"But I want to do *one* more exercise!" insisted the vampire.

"Hmm . . . " Mr Crustscrubber tugged at his moustache. "All right, we could do a couple of exercises with the yellow clothes, if you like."

"Y-you can't!" stuttered Tony.

Mr Crustscrubber looked at him in surprise. "Why not?"

"I – the bag of yellow clothes, I've left it at home, in my cupboard."

"In your cupboard?" snorted the Little Vampire. "Why do I bother to bring you with me if you've got a memory like a Swiss cheese – only with more holes!"

"I'm sorry," said Tony, sounding embarrassed.

"You're sorry? Is that all?" growled the vampire. "My treatment's going to be put back by weeks because of you – weeks!"

"Now, you are being a bit unreasonable, Rupert," Mr Crustscrubber interrupted. "Anyone can forget things. And to say that your treatment is being put back by weeks is a bit of an exaggeration, to put it mildly."

The Little Vampire's mouth twisted unpleasantly, but he said nothing.

"And in any case," went on Mr Crustscrubber in a soothing tone of voice, "we don't need the bag of clothes, as you'll see in a minute, Rupert!"

He nodded to the vampire and with a mysterious expression on his face opened a drawer of his desk – just a fraction, so that neither Tony nor Rudolph could see what was inside.

"Do you like music?" he asked.

"Yes!" answered the vampire.

"Then listen to this for a minute!" Mr Crustscrubber fumbled in the drawer, and at once the soft, rather metallic sound of tinkling music could be heard.

It was a tune Tony recognized. He listened, and suddenly he knew the song. It was "The sun has got his hat on . . . "

Mr Crustscrubber would have to choose *that* song for the Little Vampire! he thought, looking at Rudolph nervously.

But the vampire was leaning back in his armchair, and seemed to be listening, entranced.

"Do you like this music?" asked Mr Crustscrubber.

"Yes!" said the vampire. "It'd be just right for me and Olga!"

"Do you know the song?"

"No, why?"

"It's called, 'The sun has got his hat on!' "

"The . . . sun has got his hat on?" The vampire gave a groan.

"Yes. Don't get upset by the title!" Mr Crustscrubber made another movement in the drawer, and the song began all over again.

"Just listen to the music!" he said in his deep, relaxing voice. "You are completely relaxed, and you are just listening to the music!"

The Little Vampire leaned back and shut his eyes.

"Now I'm going to sing the words quietly along with the music," announced Mr Crustscrubber.

"Oh, no!" murmured Tony.

But Mr Crustscrubber had begun to sing softly:

The sun has got his hat on.
Hip-hip-hip hooray!
The sun has got his hat on
And he's coming out today!

To Tony's amazement, in spite of the mention of "sun" and "day", the Little Vampire just lay quietly.

Just For You

As Mr Crustscrubber sang, he watched the Little Vampire closely, and with some concern, it seemed to Tony. But Rudolph kept his eyes closed and showed no signs of resistance or anxiety.

"Would you like to know where the music is coming from, Rupert?" asked Mr Crustscrubber, when the song had come to an end.

"No," said the Little Vampire, without opening his eyes. "But I *would* like to hear it again."

"You will be able to listen to the music as often as you like!" said the psychologist mysteriously.

"As often as I like?" repeated the Little Vampire. He opened his eyes a chink. "Well, I'd like to hear it again now!" he declared. "Why don't you begin?"

"Because *you* are going to start it!" replied Mr Crustscrubber.

"Me?" This time, the Little Vampire opened his eyes wide. "I can't sing – at least, not today."

Mr Crustscrubber smiled. "You don't have to sing, Rupert! You only have to turn it on, just as I have!"

"Turn it on?"

"Yes!" Mr Crustscrubber felt in the drawer and brought out a circular musical box, covered in a yellow velvety material. Tony held his breath. Yellow spokes protruded from the edge and a smiling face decorated the top – the musical box was meant to resemble the sun!

But Rudolph didn't seem the least shocked or anxious – instead, he seemed surprised and perhaps slightly curious.

"This dreadful yellow object makes that lovely music?" he asked in disbelief.

Mr Crustscrubber nodded. "All you have to do is turn it on, and it will play a tune – just for you!"

"Just for me?" said the Little Vampire doubtfully. "But Tony can hear it too!"

"If you like the musical box," answered Mr Crustscrubber, looking solemn and serious, "and if you would like to keep it, I will give it to you as a present."

The vampire knitted his brows suspiciously. "You're giving the music box away, just like that?"

"No," Mr Crustscrubber contradicted him. "Giving someone a present doesn't mean giving it away 'just like that'. I want you to have it as a present because it can help you overcome your fear of sunlight."

"Oh, I see!" A relieved smile flickered across the Little Vampire's face. "Now I understand."

He drummed his fingernails on the table and murmured, "If only it wasn't this sick-making yellow colour . . . But the music's really great!"

"And Olga loves music too . . . " he added after a pause.

The thought of Olga obviously settled matters. "Well," the Little Vampire declared in his usual cheeky voice, "if the musical box is good for the treatment, I'll take it!"

"Wouldn't you have taken it otherwise?" asked Mr Crustscrubber.

"No," declared the vampire grandly. "I don't take things from humans." The musical box vanished under his cloak. "With one exception . . . "

"Yes!" said Tony grimly. "With the exception of my favourite books!"

The Little Vampire smiled wryly. "Just be thankful it's only your *books* I'm after!" He laughed hoarsely. "But I'll never get bored with reading," he said, suddenly becoming serious again as he stood up. Humming the tune from the musical box, he went to the door.

"What were the words?" he asked himself. "The moon has got his hat on? Yes, that was it: The moon has got his hat on . . . " He slammed the door of the consulting room shut behind him.

"Wait a minute!" called Tony.

"Yes, wait!" said Mr Crustscrubber. With his portly figure he had difficulty in getting out from behind his desk.

Rudolph had already reached the front door by the time Mr Crustscrubber appeared at the top of the staircase. "See you next Saturday, Rupert!" he called. "And good luck with the musical box!"

"Luck?" growled the vampire. Then he grinned. "Yes, you're right," he said. "My musical box will bring me the best of luck – with Olga!" With a husky laugh, he pulled the front door open. Then he swept up in the air and sped away with swift, powerful strokes of his arms, without paying the slightest attention to Tony.

As fast as he could, Tony flew off after him, determined to tell him what he thought. Today Rudolph had really shown himself up in his worst light!

A Good Turn

After a while, the Little Vampire slowed down and turned to Tony with an admiring grin.

"Not bad," he said. "You're flying so fast you might have been at it for a hundred years."

"Oh," drawled Tony. "Just one day would do. It's not much fun, always flying home by myself."

"Is that supposed to be a complaint?" the Little Vampire snapped.

"No, a proposal," answered Tony.

"I think you've got the wrong end of the stick!" said the Little Vampire haughtily.

"More like a slap in the face!" countered Tony.

"Don't beat about the bush!" snapped the vampire. "Out with it, if you've got something to say!"

"All right then!" Tony cleared his throat. "My proposal is this: that next Saturday, I don't come with you when you go to Mr Crustscrubber."

The Little Vampire stared at him, dumbstruck. "What are you talking about?" he asked. "You've got to come with me every time!"

"That's what *you* think!" Tony's arms beat the air with a couple of powerful strokes.

"But you'd be letting me down if you didn't!" exclaimed the vampire.

"Letting you down?" Tony gave a dry laugh. "Since when? I don't *have* to come with you!"

"But I can't go without you," said the Little Vampire, in a small voice. "You can't want me to go all alone to that—"

"I don't *want* you to!" said Tony, sounding patronizing. "I'd *like* to come with you again, if . . . " He left the sentence unfinished, to keep the vampire on tenterhooks.

"If what?" cried the Little Vampire.

"If *you* will behave like a friend should!" declared Tony.

"Behave – like a friend?" For a moment it looked as though the Little Vampire wanted to go for Tony's throat. But then he suddenly seemed to realize that Tony had the upper hand.

"All right," he said through gritted teeth. "I'll behave just like a friend, if that's what you want!"

"That's what I want." Tony was enjoying his moment of triumph. "I know the first thing you can do to show me you mean it. It's the sort of good turn a friend would do!"

"And what's that?" asked the vampire warily.

"You can come all the way back to my front door with me – I mean, my window – like a real friend would!"

"This is a great start, giving me lessons in how to be a friend!" growled the vampire. However, he did fly side by side with Tony all the way to his block of flats.

"Will this do?" hissed the vampire.

"No, I'd like you to take me right to the window," declared Tony.

The Little Vampire gave a furious snort. Then he began to grin.

"Yes, gladly," he said, with exaggerated kindness, "if you will then do a good turn for *me* in return."

To make sure Tony understood what he was talking

about, he bared his needle-sharp canine teeth.

Tony felt his skin prickle with goosepimples.

"I . . . well, you don't *have* to come all the way to the window," he said hastily.

"Why not, all of a sudden?" asked the vampire.

"Um – it's not very far now," stammered Tony.

"Typical Tony Peasbody!" remarked the vampire disapprovingly. "You demand that I do *you* a good turn, but you're not up to doing even the smallest good turn for *me*! And what's more," he added, "*you're* much less of a friend than you used to be. A real friend would never have forgotten to bring the bag of clothes!" He breathed heavily, very pleased with himself, it seemed to Tony, and then flew away without a word of goodbye.

"As far as I'm concerned, you can go and see Crustscrubber by yourself in future!" Tony called after him.

An Admirer

By the following Saturday, Tony's anger had blown over. His parents had set out for a concert shortly after seven, and he waited impatiently in his room for the Little Vampire.

He had already put the bag with the yellow clothes in it by the open window. Time slipped by and there was no sign of Rudolph. Perhaps the Little Vampire was still offended? Now Tony almost regretted having accused Rudolph of not being a real friend. But at twenty to nine the Little Vampire landed on the windowsill, rather out of breath.

"Little sisters can be real pests!" he hissed.

"What do you mean?" asked Tony, rather taken aback.

"Ha! Because of Anna, I'm now going to be late for the therapy session!"

"Because of Anna?" Tony was shocked. "Has something happened?"

"Happened? Happened?" snapped the vampire. "If we don't hurry up, it *won't* happen! Come on, put your cloak on!"

"O-OK," murmured Tony, quickly pulling the vampire cloak around him and stuffing the bag under his jumper. As they flew along side by side, he asked cautiously, "What's all this about Anna?"

"Oh, just some wretched admirer!" answered the

vampire, waving a hand dismissively.

"An – admirer?" Tony felt his heart begin to pound. "Anna's got an admirer?"

The vampire gave his grating laugh. "No, she hasn't. Aunt Dorothy has! Anna's been going on about him for so long that this evening I went along with her to have a look at him."

"You . . . you've seen him?" asked Tony. Suddenly he remembered something Mr Crustscrubber had told him some time ago about his mysterious patient: that Igno von Rant was very interested in a vampire-lady. Even then, Tony had wondered if this vampire-lady could be Aunt Dorothy . . .

"What did he look like?" asked Tony huskily.

"Oh, I dunno," said the Little Vampire brusquely. "Quite small, quite thin, oily black hair . . . "

"Oily black hair?" exclaimed Tony, his voice trembling with excitement. The two most striking things about Igno von Rant were his jet-black (obviously dyed) hair slicked back with too much hair-oil, and the smell of lily of the valley which hung about him.

"Did anything else strike you?" he asked, trying hard not to show his excitement.

"Anything else?" repeated the Little Vampire, beginning to giggle. "Yes! He's a whole head shorter than Aunt Dorothy, and so he has to stand on tiptoe when he wants to – hee, hee! – kiss her!"

"What about his scent?" asked Tony. "Does he smell of anything in particular?"

The vampire shook his head. "No, not at all."

"But what's it got to do with you?" he asked suspiciously after a pause. "Has Anna taken you along to have a look at him too?"

"No. I haven't seen Anna since Sniveller's fancy-dress

party," replied Tony.

"That's true!" The Little Vampire gave a grin. "Anna's very disappointed in you, because you didn't come to her defence against Greg!"

"Is she?" asked Tony in surprise.

"Yes!" declared the Little Vampire. "When Greg made that funny little joke about her wearing woollen tights with holes in them under her dress . . . "

Tony could remember very well who had cracked the horrible joke which had made Anna run off from the fancy-dress party: it was Rudolph himself! But because he didn't want to get into an argument with the Little Vampire again, and especially not just before the visit to Mr Crustscrubber, he decided not to pursue the matter.

"This admirer," he said, "if he smells of lily of the valley, he *could* be that mysterious patient of Mr Crustscrubber's, Igno von Rant!"

"He smells quite normal though," said the Little Vampire.

"Not even a little bit sweet?" asked Tony.

"No." The vampire sniggered. "He smells almost as good as you!" he said, with a sidelong glance at Tony's cloak.

"Me?" Tony tried to look dignified. "If there's a fusty smell about this cloak, it's not my fault!"

"Fusty smell?" asked the vampire, looking pleased. "Yes, Uncle Theodore did have a lovely personal smell about him – like sulphur and bad eggs!"

"Poor Uncle Theodore," he went on after a pause. "All we have to remember him by is his scent!" He cleared his throat and pointed down at Mr Crustscrubber's house.

"We're there!"

Lights On!

When they went into the consulting room, they saw a sort of trolley standing next to Mr Crustscubber's desk. On it, Tony could make out a tall, narrow box. In the box were several glass tubes packed upright.

"What's that?" asked the Little Vampire, approaching the box hesitantly.

"That's equipment for a light."

"A light?"

"Yes. It has an umbrella which reflects a very strong light, almost as bright as daylight."

"Daylight?" exclaimed the vampire. "But— " He didn't finish the sentence, but gave a weak groan.

"It is only artificial light," Mr Crustscrubber soothed him. "This equipment can't harm you at all, Rupert!"

"How do you know?" hissed the vampire.

"I know because I've tried it," replied Mr Crustscrubber. "My other patient, Igno von Rant, swears by the effect this light has!"

"Really?" This seemed to have convinced the Little Vampire.

"I hope you have brought your sunglasses with you!" said Mr Crustscrubber.

"The bag!" demanded the Little Vampire. "Have you got the bag?"

"Yes," growled Tony, annoyed by the vampire's rude tone of voice.

"Let's have it then!" Now the vampire was grinning. Turning to Mr Crustscrubber, he said arrogantly, "I really read the riot act to Tony, you know. He won't forget anything again in a hurry."

Tony pressed his lips together angrily. Pulling the bag roughly from under his jumper he gave it to the vampire. Immediately, Rudolph began fumbling around inside. Then a shudder ran over him.

"Yuk! So much yellow!" he croaked, and with a gesture of disgust, he held the bag out to Tony. "*You* find it!" Tony didn't move.

"Come on!" snapped the vampire.

Mr Crustscrubber, who could see quite well that another fight was brewing, cleared his throat.

"Shall I look in the bag for you?" he offered.

After a short search, he found the sunglasses. He held them out to the Little Vampire, who took them reluctantly and held them at arm's length with his tapering fingers.

"There, now sit in the armchair and relax!" said Mr Crustscrubber – sounding unusually determined, Tony thought. Rudolph growled something and let himself down into the wide armchair. As he did so, he made a face as though he had bitten into a lemon – no, much worse than that, a clove of garlic!

Tony, who as usual had to put up with the hard, uncomfortable wooden chair, watched the vampire half in amusement, half with concern. He wasn't sure whether the vampire's dislike of the glasses was just pretence. After all, they were only a bit of black plastic with extra-dark lenses!

"And now you will relax, Rupert!" Tony heard the psychologist's voice. "You are quite still, and you will let your muscles become slack, totally relaxed . . . "

"I can't do that with these disgusting glasses in my hand!" growled the vampire.

"Yes you can!" Mr Crustscrubber commanded. "You will let yourself become completely loose . . . That's right . . . Concentrate on this feeling of being relaxed . . . Now you are wonderfully peaceful . . . And now, slowly, you are going to put on the sunglasses . . . "

As if Mr Crustscrubber had hypnotized the vampire with his relaxation exercises, Rudolph lifted his right arm and set the sunglasses on his nose.

"Very good!" Mr Crustscrubber praised him. "You are now completely relaxed, Rupert . . . You can hardly feel the glasses . . . They are there, but they don't bother you at all . . . You feel completely slack and relaxed . . . "

The Little Vampire gave a sigh. He did indeed seem to be deeply relaxed; even his long, thin hands, which always seemed to be moving, lay still and relaxed on the arms of the chair.

It seemed like a marvel to Tony. He remembered what Mr Crustscrubber had said at the beginning of the treatment: if they worked at it together, he and Rudolph might be able to bring about a miracle.

"And now we are going to switch on the lights," Mr Crustscrubber announced. "You will shut your eyes and relax . . . "

Tony had expected the Little Vampire to react to the switching on of the lights with fear, maybe even panic. But the vampire remained where he was, and not one word of protest came from his narrow, rather bloodless-looking lips.

"Have you closed your eyes?" Mr Crustscrubber wanted to make sure.

"Yes."

"Good. Now stay quite relaxed, Rupert . . . "

Tony watched in excitement as Mr Crustscrubber pressed a switch which was fixed to the side of the box. For a second, nothing happened, but then the glass tubes lit up and bathed the consulting room in an extraordinarily bright, intensive light.

For a moment, Tony was almost blinded. He squeezed his eyes shut and blinked.

The light reminded him of the infra-red lamp at home, which gave off the same sort of penetrating light. But the light from this equipment wasn't red, it was white.

Mr Crustscrubber pushed the trolley with the light on it nearer to the armchair.

It was horrible to see, Rudolph sitting there, completely motionless, the light reflecting in the dark lenses of his sunglasses. It was like a horror film Tony had once seen!

"Good, and now you are going to open your eyes and, staying quite relaxed, you will look straight at the light!" ordered Mr Crustscrubber. "You are nice and slack . . . Completely relaxed . . . Now, turn your eyes on the light . . . And stay still, quite still . . . "

The vampire moved his head, but Tony couldn't see through the reflection in the sunglasses whether Rudolph really had opened his eyes.

At that moment, there came a knock at the door.

All This Secrecy

Tony jumped. Even Mr Crustscrubber looked disconcerted, but he quickly pulled himself together and said to the Little Vampire in his slow, deliberate voice, "Sit still, Rupert. Sit still and keep calm and relaxed. Now close your eyes . . . You have closed your eyes and you are completely slack . . . yes, that's it . . . I will be straight back!"

Mr Crustscrubber walked over to the door on his squeaky soles. There he spoke – in a rather agitated manner, it seemed to Tony – to his wife. As Tony had already guessed, it was she who had knocked on the door.

Tony listened, but could only pick up a couple of fragments of their conversation. "Much too soon!" he heard Mr Crustscrubber say, and, "That would happen at the crucial moment."

He studied the Little Vampire, who was sitting motionless in the armchair. It was impossible to tell whether Rudolpoh had his eyes open or closed. As Tony continued to watch him, Mr Crustscrubber came back.

The psychologist stopped beside Tony, laid a hand on his shoulder and said in a whisper: "You're wanted on the telephone, Tony."

"Me? On the telephone?" repeated Tony. "But it hasn't rung," he said, pointing to the telephone on Mr Crustscrubber's desk.

"Sssh! Not so loud!" replied Mr Crustscrubber, looking over at Rudolph in concern. "My wife took the call in her office," he explained quietly.

"Oh, I see," murmured Tony.

With a worried glance at the vampire, Tony left the room. Rudolph was still sitting motionless, his face turned towards the light, almost as though he had fallen asleep.

Mrs Crustscrubber was waiting in the hall. Her hair was tied up in a bun, as usual. But this time she was wearing large glittering earrings and a long string of pearls.

Nodding to Tony in a friendly way, she led the way to her "office" – a long, narrow room next to the front door.

"The telephone call," said Tony hoarsely, "who is it?"

Mrs Crustscrubber turned to him smiling, and said nothing.

With all this secrecy, it must be someone very special! thought Tony. But who? He hadn't told anyone, not even his parents, that he was going to be at Mr Crustscrubber's tonight. Then, suddenly, he had an idea: Anna!

She must have found out from Rudolph that he had an appointment with the psychologist and that Tony would be going with him. Tony felt his heart beat faster.

Anna was probably going to tell him off for his behaviour at Sniveller's fancy dress party. Tony had tried to run after her, but Rudolph had stopped him. Even so, ought he to apologize to her?

Mrs Crustscrubber opened the door to her room and nodded to him to come in. Hesitantly, with a feeling of unease, Tony went inside.

His gaze fell on the window. That was where Igno von Rant had been standing that evening when Tony had glanced inside as he made his next appointment. That time, the room had been filled with a horribly sweet scent of lily of the valley, mixed with the unmistakable smell of decay. The thought of that second meeting with Igno von Rant sent a shiver down his spine.

"Make yourself comfortable, Tony!" Mrs Crustscrubber pointed to a thickly padded brown armchair. She sat down at the desk, on a hard upright chair.

Tony studied the armchair. He could have sworn that old thing hadn't been there last time.

He was just about to sit down when he saw the telephone and he gave a start. The receiver wasn't lying beside it: it was in its place on the hook!

Without a word, he looked at Mrs Crustscrubber.

"Sit down, Tony!" she said. She sounded friendly but determined.

Puzzled, Tony sat down.

"The telephone— " he began. "Someone must have put the receiver back . . . "

And now Anna's going to be really furious with me! was the thought that shot through his head.

"I'll explain everything," answered Mrs Crustscrubber. "You do of course know about the course of treatment that my husband has developed against phobias."

"Y-yes."

"My husband has been working on the treatment for many years," she went on in a solemn voice. "And now, after such a long time of self-denial, he is at last standing on the threshold!" She paused.

"On the threshold?" repeated Tony, not sure what she meant.

"Yes! Soon it will be proved that his treatment really works," said Mrs Crustscrubber. "And I hope you will be able to help us!"

She stopped and smiled at Tony. She was being a bit too free and easy, Tony thought. He looked over at the telephone. "The call . . . I mean, who wanted to talk to me?"

"Just listen to me for a moment longer," said Mrs Crustscrubber, without answering his question. "In this critical phase that has just begun," she explained, "everything depends on my husband being able to work with Rupert under the best of all possible conditions. You see that, don't you?"

Tony nodded.

"Yes. That's why I called you out of the consultation this evening – so that you could wait for the end of the session in my study. Although I did come for you a bit too early, as it happens . . . " She cleared her throat.

"Anyway," she went on, taking two comics, a bar of chocolate and a bag of sweets out of a drawer, "these should sweeten the waiting time for you."

"Now I'm beginning to understand . . . " Tony took a deep breath. "All that rubbish about a telephone call was just a trick!"

"No, I wouldn't call it that," Mrs Crustscrubber countered. "It was a necessary step in the treatment."

"A step in the treatment?"

"Yes. Rupert has got to learn that he can manage the treatment all by himself. Only when he has discovered that will he succeed in overcoming his sun phobia totally!"

Shut Out

Tony said nothing. He was furious that Mr Crustscrubber and his wife should have resorted to such a trick!

He could certainly understand that it was important – perhaps even a matter of life or death – for the Little Vampire to get through the treatment on his own and without Tony's help. Even so when he thought of Rudolph sitting in the consulting room doing the exercises with the sun tan oil and the yellow tracksuit, Tony felt he had been deceived – shut out.

Mrs Crustscrubber seemed to be considering his disappointment. "I can well imagine what's going through your mind, Tony," she said. "But just think of Rupert for a moment, and how lovely his life will be once he has overcome his fear of sunlight!"

"Life?" Tony grinned weakly.

"How forlorn, how bleak his existence must have been up till now!" continued Mrs Crustscrubber with feeling. "Away from the light of the sun, sentenced to everlasting darkness. Believe me, if the treatment is successful, Rupert will be very, very grateful to you!"

"Grateful? To me?" said Tony doubtfully.

"Of course he will!" Mrs Crustscrubber nodded confidently. There was a pause.

Tony glanced over at the door. He was tempted to get up and go back into the consulting room. After all, he had brought Mr Crustscrubber and the Little Vampire together. He had even paid for the sun cream and the sun tan oil out of his own pocket money! And now he suddenly seemed to be neither wanted nor needed . . . "Persona non grappa" or something like it – that was one of his father's favourite expressions, anyhow!

"Would you like a sweet?" he heard Mrs Crustscrubber say.

"No," he growled.

"Or a piece of chocolate?" She rustled the wrapper.

"No, thank you. I'm not hungry. And I don't want to read either!" he managed to get in before she could speak, glancing at the comics.

"All right then," Mrs Crustscrubber seemed unconcerned. "Then we will just sit here and wait till Rupert has finished the session." She looked at her watch. "Anyhow, it won't last very much longer."

Tony didn't answer. He suddenly had a peculiar feeling. Could there be another reason for his sudden exclusion from the therapy session? For instance, did Mr Crustscrubber want to rid himself of a dangerous witness? He strained his ears to see whether he could hear any sound from the consulting room, but then he remembered just how thickly padded its door was.

Padded . . . He looked at the brown armchair he was sitting in. Wasn't it strange that there had only been an uncomfortable chair for him in the psychologist's room, whereas here was this cosy one all ready for him? It all seemed to have been . . . pre-arranged, as though Mr Crustscrubber and his wife had worked out a plan together. The comics and the sweets bore this out, and strengthened Tony's suspicions.

His glance lingered on Mrs Crustscrubber distrustfully. She was playing with her pearl necklace and seemed to be lost in her own thoughts.

Tony would have liked to jump up and do something. Terrible things might be happening to the Little Vampire in the consulting room while he sat about doing nothing . . . But what other choice did he have? If he heard any sort of alarming noise, he would definitely act!

But the flat, the house – everything seemed to have fallen into a stillness worthy of the Sleeping Beauty!

The longer Tony strained his ears in this mysterious quiet, the more nervous and restless he became. When he finally heard steps in the hallway, it was almost like a release. Without stopping to think, he ran to the door. He tore it open – and there stood the Little Vampire.

Stupid Remarks

"Rudolph!" he said happily – and then hesitated.

The Little Vampire was still wearing the sunglasses and looked exhausted.

"What's the matter with your eyes?" asked Tony, shocked.

The vampire scowled, as though Tony's concern annoyed him.

"Nothing!" he hissed.

"Nothing?" repeated Tony. "Why the glasses then?"

"Rupert likes the sunglasses so much that he doesn't want to take them off again!" said Mr Crustscrubber. He stood a couple of paces behind the vampire, wearing a very contented look on his face.

"A resounding success!" he said delightedly. "Quite extraordinary. I am really proud of Rupert!"

The vampire grinned, looking flattered.

"Did everything work?" asked Tony.

"Yes, brilliantly," replied Mr Crustscrubber. "But now Rupert is very tired."

"Not *very* tired," the Little Vampire corrected him, laughing huskily. "After all, I'm renowned for my strong nerves."

"Oh, are you?" said Tony mischievously.

"You just can't bear it when someone says something nice about *me*, can you?" hissed the Little Vampire scornfully. "Huh! The session went a thousand times better without you! I could really concentrate properly, with no-one wandering about and putting me off with stupid remarks!" He snorted noisily, as if to underline his words. "And by the way," he went on in an even louder voice, "in future, I won't need you to come with me any more, Tony Peasbody! Next time, I shall visit Mr Crustscrubber on my own!" With that, he turned round and vanished into the hall.

"Wait, Rupert!" said Mr Crustscrubber, hurrying after him.

Tony followed them slowly, boiling with rage. He felt a real fool. *He* had been thinking and worrying about the Little Vampire, wanting to help him, stand by him through danger . . . and what did the vampire do? As soon as he had the chance, he dropped Tony. He didn't seem to care about him in the least. The Little Vampire was just ungrateful and unfaithful – he only thought about himself.

By the time Tony reached the front door, he wasn't at all surprised to see that Mr Crustscrubber was standing there alone. The psychologist was obviously in a very good mood. He turned to Tony with a broad smile and announced with great emotion: "That was quite an extraordinary consultation. It has given me cause for great hope."

"Really?" said Tony dully.

He didn't feel like listening while Mr Crustscrubber sang the Little Vampire's praises!

"Well, you obviously don't need me any more," he said.

"Don't need you?" repeated Mr Crustscrubber, pretending to sound indignant. "Of course we do! In a way, you're the most important person!"

"Me?" Tony gave a dry laugh.

He had already heard that speech about being the "most important person" – on his first visit to the psychologist's practice. It might have been true then, but today Tony felt it was just a pitiful attempt to win him over, away from his feelings of irritation and disappointment. "Good night," he said, marching off.

"Tony, you've forgotten your bag!" he heard Mr Crustscrubber call after him.

But Tony gave no reply. What did he care about the sun tan oil, the yellow socks or the headband? Without turning round once, he set off down the narrow, dark pathway. In the shelter of the bushes, he spread out his arms under his cloak, moved them up and down strongly, and flew away.

Every Night I'm Out With Tony!

Tony landed on the stone ledge outside his window, feeling somewhat exhausted. The flat was in darkness – he had already made sure of that as he flew around. At least he was spared his parents' anger this evening!

He had once again locked his bedroom door from the inside, but his mother still refused to accept that he could lock his door for the sake of privacy, even though Mr Crustscrubber would back him up. All she could talk about was a "lack of trust" and "secret goings-on". But "secret goings-on" was correct when you were the friend of a vampire!

A friend . . . ? Tony bit his lip.

No, after what had happened this evening, he wasn't sure he could call the Little Vampire his friend any more. He pushed the window open and slipped down from the sill into his room.

As Tony's feet touched the floor, music began to play. It was "The sun has got his hat on" – the song from the musical box.

"Rudolph!" he cried happily.

The Little Vampire must have realized he'd behaved disgracefully when they parted. He wouldn't apologize – he never did – but perhaps he wanted to make up in his own way. But the Little Vampire said nothing . . . There was only the sound of the bright, tinkling music.

Tony frowned. The vampire was sitting on his bed

with his black cloak pulled over his head.

"Rudolph?" Tony repeated, a little more cautiously this time.

"No!" came the gruff reply.

Suddenly Tony understood. "Anna!" he exclaimed.

The bedside lamp was switched on, and Tony saw Anna, who was pushing back her cloak with a sulky look on her face.

"I . . . I thought it was Rudolph!" stuttered Tony. He couldn't think of anything else to say.

"I realise that!" Anna snapped.

"I . . . the music . . . " Tony gulped.

He took off the vampire cloak awkwardly and hung it over the chair by his desk.

"You know, the musical box . . . I thought it was Rudolph's."

"It is," Anna replied. "I borrowed it."

"Borrowed it?" repeated Tony, glad to see that Anna didn't look quite so cross any more.

"Yes," she said.

"And I've thought up some words for the music!" she added brightly. Then suddenly her face took on its distrustful look again. "But if you can only ever think about Rudolph, you won't want to hear them!"

"Oh, I do!" Tony reassured her, adding, "Rudolph and I – we're not friends any more – at least, not best friends."

"Aren't you?" This news seemed to please Anna. Chuckling delightedly she announced, "All right then, this is how it goes!" She opened the musical box and began to sing:

Every night I'm out with Tony
Hip-hip-hip hooray!

Every night I'm out with Tony
And we're going off to play!

"Well? What do you think?" she asked expectantly.

"I – " Tony cleared his throat. "*Every* night's a bit of an exaggeration," he said, just for something to say. "We haven't seen each other for at least two weeks!"

"Exactly!" declared Anna, fiddling with her hair, which was looking amazingly well brushed. She must have taken a lot of trouble to get it looking so sleek and shining.

"I was very angry with you, you see," she said.

"Were you?" asked Tony, his heart beating.

She blushed. "I'm *still* very angry with you," she corrected herself hastily. "Because you let them all laugh at me – Greg, Rudolph and Sniveller! What's more, you just stood there looking when I ran away!"

"No, that's not true!" Tony contradicted her. "I ran after you!"

"Did you?"

"Yes! But Rudolph grabbed me by the cloak and said you'd scratch my eyes out if I tried to catch up with you."

"He said what?" exclaimed Anna crossly. "I'd scratch *your* eyes out?"

Again, her expression changed, and she said very gently, "I'd never hurt you – not even the tiniest bit!"

Now it was Tony's turn to blush.

She gazed at his neck. "Not even the tiniest bit!" she added with a meaningful smile.

Chaperone

"If I'd known you'd tried to come after me," she went on in her normal, rather husky voice, "then of course I would have come to see you much sooner! Although – " she glanced towards the window, "there's been such a lot going on at home recently."

"What happened?"

"Hasn't Rudolph told you that his Olga's coming back?" Anna retorted.

"What? You mean it isn't just a rumour?" murmured Tony, taken aback.

Anna sighed. "Unfortunately not."

"But this messenger, Richard the Resentful, doesn't really exist, does he?" asked Tony, confused.

"Of course he does!" replied Anna, and there was a note of pride in her voice. "He keeps up the links between all the different vampire families scattered throughout Europe!"

Tony had gone pale. "And I thought the whole business about Olga coming back was just a rumour Greg had spread around to annoy Rudolph . . . "

Anna shook her head. "It looks as though Olga will be arriving in four or five weeks' time."

"Oh, no!" Tony couldn't stop himself.

"You can say that again!" agreed Anna.

"And then there's this new admirer . . . " she went on darkly.

Tony pricked up his ears. "You mean Aunt Dorothy's?"

"Oh, do you know about him?"

"Yes, Rudolph told me."

"He's a boring old boot!" Anna complained. "And almost every night *I* have to go with them and listen to him flirting away with her!"

"*You* have to go with them?"

"Yes, as a chaperone."

"A what?"

"Don't you know what that is?" Anna giggled. "A chaperone's someone who keeps an eye on them to make sure they behave properly!"

"Why should she need to keep an eye on them?"

"To make sure Aunt Dorothy remains an honourable widow!" explained Anna, tittering.

Then, growing serious once more, she continued, "If only you knew how dreary it is, being a chaperone! Night after night, the two of them sit on the park bench and bill and coo like a pair of turtle doves! And then they go for hour-long walks! Just imagine, Tony: two vampires *walking* around together!" Anna put a hand to her head and groaned. "Luckily it's Greg's turn for the next two nights – thanks be to Dracula!"

"Is he going to be their chaperone?" asked Tony.

"Well, not really – after all, he's no lady!" replied Anna, laughing so loudly that Tony glanced at the door. Then he remembered they were alone in the flat!

The Real Reason

"But we haven't talked about the real reason for my visit," Anna said, looking tenderly at Tony.

"The real reason?" repeated Tony.

He'd just been on the point of asking the name of Aunt Dorothy's admirer. But now Anna would be bound to scold him for not being interested in finding out the real reason why she had come, so he kept the question for later.

Anna gazed at him from large, glowing eyes. "It's about the treatment!"

"The treatment?"

"Yes! Rudolph's told me so much about it," she said, then quickly corrected herself. "Well, not *so* much – you know what he's like! But he's . . . he's given lots of very promising hints. And I was wondering whether I might follow the treatment myself!"

"Really?"

"Well, my canine teeth are still growing— " Anna laughed in embarrassment. "I tried so hard to stop them getting any longer."

"But willpower alone isn't enough," she declared after a pause, sighing sadly. "You just can't go against your own nature, or so my grandmother, Sabina the Sinister, says. *She's* very pleased about my teeth." Anna gave a shamefaced giggle.

"But unfortunately, my nature isn't as simple as my

grandmother thinks!" she said. "After all, it's my nature to be attracted to *you*, and I'm just as unsuccessful in going against it as far as you're concerned! And since you don't seem to want to become a vampire . . . "

"N-no, I don't!" said Tony hastily.

"Well, that's why I thought: if you don't want to become like me, I ought to try to become like you!"

"You? Like me?" said Tony in surprise.

"Yes, with this treatment! If it works, we could be together much more. We could go to school together – oh, we could do thousands of things! And Rudolph says the treatment can work wonders!"

"Mr Crustscrubber, the psychologist, says that," said Tony, strangely moved by Anna's words, which were spoken with such feeling.

"That's even better," said Anna. "Then at least it's worth a try, don't you think?" She looked at him inquiringly.

Tony nodded. "Yes!"

"Well, I'm going to have a go – if you'll help me," Anna declared.

"Me?"

"Yes! You can tell me all about the treatment!"

"I can only tell you what *I* know," Tony rejoined.

Anna smiled. "Yes, everything you know!"

Tony coughed a couple of times.

Shyly, he sat down next to Anna on the bed, and in a husky voice began to tell her about the sun tan oil, the sun cream, the yellow clothing, the sunglasses, the lighting equipment, the armchair to relax in. Then he described a couple of Mr Crustscrubber's relaxation exercises as well as he could.

The more he told her, the more excited Anna became.

"But that sounds fantastic!" she exclaimed when Tony had finished. "Do you think I could have a trial session myself?"

"I'm sure you could," Tony told her.

"But I'd rather just watch at first," said Anna, after a little thought. "Do you think that would be possible?"

"Hmm— " Tony hesitated. "I'd have to ask Mr Crustscrubber." Then suddenly he remembered something. "Next Saturday, when Rudolph has his appointment, we – you and me – we could fly to Mr Crustscrubber's and peep in from outside."

"What do you mean, from outside?"

"We could look through the window."

"Oh, through the window!" said Anna, giggling. "Oh yes, let's!"

She was so pleased she put her arms round Tony and gave him a quick kiss.

Still giggling, she stood up. "I must fly!"

"Already?"

"Yes, I must go and see whether Greg's doing his duty." She gave Tony another heartfelt look.

"See you Saturday!" she said.

Cautiously, Tony felt his cheek, but Anna's lips had left no mark, not the "tiniest bit"!

Life Would be Boring without Vampires

The following Saturday, Anna landed on Tony's windowsill shortly after nine o'clock.

"Good evening, Tony!" she said with a tender smile.

She was wearing her dark red headband again, and looked amazingly neat and tidy – for a vampire.

"Hallo, Anna," Tony said huskily.

"Are you ready?" she asked.

Tony nodded. He wrapped the vampire cloak around him and climbed on to the windowsill.

Outside, Anna whispered, "Do you know which way we have to fly?"

"Yes," he replied.

The bright moonlight fell on her face and made her large eyes glimmer. She really did look very sweet . . .

Tony quickly turned his gaze away. He was afraid he might forget to move his arms up and down if he went on looking at Anna any longer.

"Isn't it a beautiful night?" he heard her ask. "Just the night for moonlight bathing!"

"B-bathing?" said Tony. "But I thought we were going to Mr Crustscrubber's!"

"Yes," said Anna softly. "It was only an idea, to go for a moonlight bathe. And life would be very boring if we didn't have ideas, don't you think?"

"Yes," Tony agreed. But it would be even more boring without vampires! he added to himself as an afterthought. Although "life" wasn't quite the right expression, as far as Anna and Rudolph were concerned. Even if Anna did risk everything to become more like him.

After a while, Tony slowed down.

"Here we are!" he said, his voice automatically dropping to a whisper. "Can you see that big house with the bushes over there? Mr Crustscrubber has his practice on the ground floor."

"On the ground floor?" repeated Anna. "What a pity!"

'Why?" asked Tony.

"Because we don't need our cloaks!" she said, looking disappointed.

"We'll need them to fly home," Tony replied. "Otherwise we'd have to sit on a bus for hours."

"I'd love to sit on a bus with you for hours – or even better, for ever!" said Anna.

Tony didn't answer. He steered towards the little front garden and landed behind the rose bushes. Anna followed him.

"Where will Rudolph be?" she asked softly.

Tony studied the front windows. To the right of the front door, he could make out six windows, which he presumed all belonged to Mr Crustscrubber's practice. The first four were dark, but he could see a light behind the last two.

He tried to remember how many windows there were in Mr Crustscrubber's consulting room. He thought there were two . . .

"The last two," he whispered. "They must be the consulting room."

"It's lucky the psychologist doesn't have roller blinds!" remarked Anna. "Just those thick lace curtains – yuk!"

"Don't you like lace?" asked Tony in surprise. He thought of how delighted Anna had been with the old tattered lace dress she had found in the ruins in the Vale of Doom.

"Yes, I do," said Anna. "But it's the most terrible waste for curtains. In fact, any sort of curtains are a waste!" she went on. "It would be much easier if humans didn't have curtains or blinds or anything at the windows!" She giggled.

"But lace curtains are see-through," said Tony. "Anyway, if it really is the consulting room, we'll be in luck!"

"Why?"

"Well, because the wall's built up a bit under the windows. We can sit there quite comfortably and look into the room."

"Yes, you're right." Anna spread out her cloak, moved her arms a couple of times, and landed in front of the left-hand window.

Tony flew after her and landed on the right-hand windowsill.

"Tailor-made – no, tailor-built for us!" said Anna.

Tony glanced quickly over at the street. But the windows were in the shadow of a tall pine tree, so that anyone going by would be unable to see them.

Noises and Smells

"I can see Rudolph!" whispered Anna excitedly. "He's lying down, and his eyes are closed. Do you think he's fainted?"

"Fainted?" repeated Tony. "I expect it's one of the relaxation exercises."

"What do you mean, you expect? I thought you *knew* what Rudolph was doing in there!"

"Can't see," Tony grinned. "Mr Crustscrubber's big bottom's blocking my view!"

"Then come over here by me!"

"Isn't it too narrow for two of us?"

"Too narrow?" Anna laughed. "It could never be narrow enough for us two!"

"If you think so . . . " Tony felt embarrassed, but he jumped over next to her. Now he noticed the slight smell of decay which hung about her beneath her "Eternal Love" rose perfume. Never narrow enough . . . Even if Anna was the nicest girl Tony had ever met, she was still a vampire and her wish to be a closer and closer friend would never come true.

As if Anna had read his thoughts, she looked at him and smiled tenderly. Hurriedly, Tony turned his eyes away.

He saw the armchair, and the Little Vampire stretched out on it, obviously totally relaxed and at peace.

"Isn't it strange?" said Anna quietly. "That

psychologist could do anything to him! And Rudolph has completely surrendered . . . "

"But Mr Crustscrubber only wants to try out his treatment on Rudolph," Tony tried to calm her. "He isn't particularly interested in vampires. He only wanted to meet you because you've got such a strong fear of sunlight – sun phobia he calls it. Mr Crustscrubber would never do anything to Rudolph or to you."

"Do you think so?" Anna didn't sound convinced.

"Yes!" Tony assured her, though he too felt slightly uneasy watching the Little Vampire through the window like this. He wouldn't be able to do anything if there was an emergency! On the other hand, it had been Rudolph's idea to ban Tony from any more sessions!

"Why should lying down do any good?" asked Anna. "After all, Rudolph spends the whole day in his coffin!"

"Mr Crustscrubber's probably talking to him," said Tony. "Or reading something to him."

"Reading to him? How's that going to help?"

"Perhaps it's a story about the sun!"

"About the sun?" Anna laughed scornfully. "Rudolph wouldn't be lying so still if it was, I can tell you that!"

"It might be, though!" Tony insisted. "That's the funny thing about the exercises. You're brought closer and closer to the things that make you frightened. But because you're completely relaxed, they suddenly don't seem so frightening any more."

"Oh, I see . . . " Anna breathed in and out. "What's going to happen now?"

Mr Crustscrubber had got out of his swivel chair and was holding out the yellow socks and headband to the Little Vampire, who by now had opened his eyes.

"I bet Rudolph's got to make himself look smart!" Tony replied.

"Make himself smart?"

"Yes!"

The Little Vampire stretched the headband over his wild mane of hair, grimacing. But he tugged it determinedly over his forehead, pulling out the strands of hair that were caught underneath.

"Yuk!" said Anna in disgust. "Vampires should never wear yellow!"

"But it's all part of the sun phobia," explained Tony, though he had to admit she was right: the yellow headband looked quite revolting against the vampire's chalk-white skin and dark-rimmed eyes – quite different from Anna's dark red headband.

"Do you think *I'd* have to wear a yellow headband like that if I followed the treatment?" she asked.

Tony nodded, trying desperately not to laugh, as the Little Vampire began to undress. First he took off his strange black shoes, which were made of fabric, then his woolly tights and Tony saw, to his amazement, that he was wearing *two* pairs.

"Don't look!" said Anna.

"Why not?" asked Tony, puzzled.

"Because I don't want you to see the shabby old things we have to put up with!" she declared.

"I don't care!" Tony said. "It's all part of the therapy, and I *must* know what happens next in the treatment."

"No!" Anna insisted. "I'll tell you when you can look again!"

Tony turned his head away. As his gaze travelled over the street, he imagined what a smell there must be coming from Rudolph's feet and his ancient, holey tights! What a good thing there was a thick pane of glass between them! he thought. It blocks out noises and . . . smells!

"There, you can look now!" he heard Anna say.

Tony turned round, and almost exclaimed out loud. The Little Vampire was lying back in the relaxing chair with his ghastly white legs completely bare. On his feet were the yellow socks, at least one size too big for him. And he was still wearing the yellow headband. The sight made Tony shudder, but at the same time he wanted to burst out laughing.

"And you call that making himself look smart!" said Anna.

"But it's working!" retorted Tony. "Rudolph's looking very happy!"

Blind with Love

"Yes, he does look happy," Anna admitted. The Little Vampire had closed his eyes again, and seemed to be dreaming.

"He's probably thinking of Olga," said Tony with a grin.

"Don't talk about Olga!" hissed Anna. "It's bad enough that she'll be here soon!"

"Do you know when?"

"It's supposed to be in four or five weeks," said Anna coldly. "But even if she didn't turn up for another *eight* weeks it would still be much too soon, if you ask me!"

I hope it *is* eight weeks! thought Tony. Or even better, twelve! Then the Little Vampire would have time to repeat Mr Crustscrubber's exercises so often that he really would have learned them. If Olga arrived too soon, Rudolph would probably go out in the sunlight before he was ready, simply because he was so blind with love. The thought made Tony's blood run cold.

At that moment Mr Crustscrubber began to push the trolley with the lighting equipment over to the relaxing chair, while the Little Vampire made a great show of putting on the dark glasses.

Then, before Tony had a chance to warn Anna, the light bulbs lit up.

"Aaagh! What's that?" Anna gave a shrill cry and held her hands in front of her eyes.

"It's the lights," explained Tony, startled.

Anna blinked. "Why does he need that dreadful bright light?"

"Rudolph has to look at it for a while – with the sunglasses on, of course – so that his eyes get used to bright light."

"But I haven't got sunglasses on!" cried Anna.

"You'll have a pair if you follow the treatment," Tony assured her.

"But what about now?" said Anna, her voice quivering with agitation. "I've just looked at the light through the window, and my eyes weren't protected at all!" She sobbed.

Tony felt guilty. It had never occurred to him that Anna might be in danger too!

"Don't you remember that disaster with the photo?" asked Anna, on the verge of tears.

"Yes, I do." Tony remembered very well how his parents had come home unexpectedly while they were holding a Transylvanian evening, and how his father had hit upon the fatal idea of taking a photograph of Anna and Tony together.

Anna had suffered terrible headaches and blurred vision for weeks afterwards, because of the harsh bright light of the camera flash.

"But this light isn't quite as bright as that other one!" Tony assured her.

When Anna didn't reply, he asked worriedly, "Are your eyes hurting already?"

"I don't know," she murmured, blinking once or twice. "No," she said. "It seems to be all right . . . "

"And I can see *you* quite clearly!" she added. With these words she cheered up again and began to smile.

You're Different

"I – I should have warned you about the lights," said Tony in a small voice. "I just simply didn't think— " He coughed in embarrassment. "I'm sorry."

Anna's head was lowered.

"Is Rudolph still looking at the light?" she asked softly. It sounds as though she's almost forgiven me! thought Tony. He glanced into the room. "Yes. Rudolph's sitting just where he was."

"And Mr Crustscrubber?"

"He's talking to him."

"Is that all?"

"I think Mr Crustscrubber's going to switch off the lights."

"Switch them off?" Anna sighed. "I hope so!"

"I could buy you a pair of sunglasses too," suggested Tony.

"Me?" Anna passed a hand over her eyes. "It's too late for that now."

"No, I meant for next Saturday," Tony replied. "Just in case we come back and Mr Crustscrubber uses the lights again."

"Oh, I see," said Anna. She looked cautiously at Tony and added, with a teasing smile, "Yes, if you'd like to and if your money isn't too good for that sort of thing."

"My money – too good for you?" said Tony indignantly. "Of course it isn't! Though it was too good for Rudolph!"

"What do you mean?" said Anna in surprise. At that moment the bright lights went out. Tony blinked.

"I told you Rudolph and I aren't friends any more," he explained in a whisper. At any rate, not best friends."

"Yes, I know," replied Anna, whispering too. "Because he banned you from the therapy sessions."

"And because he just uses me all the time," Tony explained.

Inside the consulting room, the Little Vampire had begun some new relaxation exercises. Tony watched as he raised his shoulders and let them drop again.

"*I'm* supposed to spend my pocket money on him," said Tony grimly. "Rudolph only thinks of himself."

"Yes, he does," Anna agreed. After a pause, she added softly, "But that's part of our nature."

"Part of your nature?"

"Yes, you see . . . " She cleared her throat with embarrassment. "None of us would survive if we didn't think of ourselves first."

"But you're different!" retorted Tony.

"Yes, perhaps!" Anna gave a shamefaced giggle. "But – I might eventually get to be like Rudolph!"

"You?"

"Mmm, yes – if I grow vampire teeth and turn into a proper vampire . . . "

Tony felt goosepimples prickle his skin and automatically moved away from Anna a fraction.

"But that's exactly why I want to follow Mr Crustscrubber's course of treatment!" Anna protested. "So that it won't happen for a very, very long time!" She looked at Tony tenderly. "Or have you changed your mind in the meantime?"

Tony knew exactly what she was referring to: his refusal to become a vampire. "Nothing will ever change

71

my mind!" he said firmly.

A shadow flitted across her face.

"Never?"

"No!"

"Well, here's another thing that won't ever change!" said Anna, with a sly little laugh. "I'm going to keep on asking if you have!"

Lumpy Stuff

Anna turned to look into the consulting room and asked, in a voice full of concern "Is Rudolph going to eat something now?"

Tony gave a start. He'd been paying more attention to Anna than to what was going on in the psychologist's room. Mr Crustscrubber had given Rudolph a tray on which lay a large, yellow lump.

"Eat?" said Tony doubtfully. The strange yellow lump didn't look very appetizing.

Or did it? He watched as the Little Vampire picked up the mysterious lump, held it under his nose and sniffed it. Then he said something to Mr Crustscrubber, and began to mould the yellow stuff into a sausage shape.

"Dough – it's dough!" said Tony excitedly.

"Dough?" said Anna, sounding puzzled. "But I thought 'dough' meant money, and that's coins and notes!"

"No, not that sort of dough!" Tony grinned. "It's playdough. You can model it into cars, houses, people . . . "

"People?" Anna giggled. "I don't think Rudolph will want to make it into people!"

She was right: the dough in the Little Vampire's bony fingers began to take on the shape of a coffin – a mini-coffin!

Tony grinned. "How very smart – a *yellow* coffin!"

The vampire seemed to have completely forgotten his dislike of the colour yellow as he moulded the playdough in his hands. Next he made two crosses and a rat. By then he had used it all up. He raised his head and looked at Mr Crustscrubber expectantly, but the psychologist shook his head with a good-natured smile.

"It looks as though Rudolph's session's finished for today," whispered Tony.

"I've had quite enough too!" Anna replied.

Tony looked at her with surprise. The exercises seemed almost like games to him, but the Little Vampire always looked completely worn out by the end of the sessions. They seemed to have had the same effect on Anna, even though she had only been watching! It must be something to do with the fact that both of them – as vampires – were completely unused to following instructions.

And then there was the mental stress of the sessions – the fear that Mr Crustscrubber might be planning some harm . . .

And lastly, Anna and Rudolph had not been used to dealing with human beings for more than a hundred and fifty years!

The Little Vampire had got up from the relaxing chair.

"Come on, let's fly," said Anna.

"Don't you want to wait for Rudolph?"

"No, it's better if he doesn't know that I was here – that *we* were here," she answered, spreading out her cloak. With a couple of powerful movements of her arms, she rose into the air.

Tony followed her, undecided as to whether or not he should wait for the Little Vampire. On the other hand, Rudolph had been so mean and unfriendly last Saturday in Mr Crustscrubber's house that he had no wish to be treated the same way again!

Enough Action for
One Evening

'Where are we flying now?" asked Tony, when he had caught up with Anna.

"Where are we flying?" she repeated rather defensively, as though she'd had enough for one evening!

I hope she doesn't just want to go back to the vault! thought Tony, who felt like doing something exciting after watching outside Mr Crustscrubber's window.

"Don't you have to go home now?" asked Anna.

"Me?" said Tony. "No!" They flew past a church tower and Tony saw that the hands on the clock stood at half past ten. His parents were at an eve-of-the-wedding party with one of his mother's colleagues, and Tony knew from experience that that kind of party went on till the early hours of the morning!

"I've got lots of time left," he explained. Then, just to tempt Anna, he added, "So if you like, we could try your moonlight bathing idea: I mean, if we can find a lake and the water isn't *too* cold."

But to his amazement, Anna shook her head. "No," she said. "I must go and think about Mr Crustscrubber and his treatment, and I need peace and quiet to do that."

Peace and quiet? That sounded suspiciously like the vault – her peaceful Sackville-Bagg vault.

"And what's more, I've got to check whether Greg really has done his duty tonight!" Anna finished.

Tony pricked up his ears.

"Greg? You mean, keeping an eye on Aunt Dorothy and her admirer?"

"Exactly!" said Anna. "We swapped turns. I ought to be snooping around Aunt Dorothy this evening, as her chaperone! But then I couldn't have flown with you to see Mr Crustscrubber. I only hope Greg hasn't run off like he did last time!"

Tony felt his heart beat faster with excitement. If Anna had to check whether Greg was with Aunt Dorothy, it could still turn into quite an exciting evening!

"Do you know where they are?" he asked.

"They were going to the water tower. On the ground floor level, there's a pub called 'The Lovesick Chestnut Tree'."

"What? They've gone to a pub?" asked Tony in disbelief.

"Not *into* the pub," replied Anna. "They're sitting outside, probably just next to the lovesick chestnut tree!"

Tony grinned. "A lovesick chestnut tree! I hope it's in love with something nice and prickly!"

"There are a couple of cosy little places to sit outside," explained Anna, giggling. "Little places among the rose bushes, like in my fairy-tale."

"Your fairy-tale?"

"Don't you remember? The story about the king's son asleep in the castle for a hundred years behind a hedge of thorns? There was only one particular princess who could get through the thorns, because she could – well, she could do something special."

"Oh, yes," said Tony. It was the story of the Sleeping Beauty, which Anna had re-written. In Anna's story the rescuer was of course a girl, and no ordinary girl either – a vampire!

"I would have been very disappointed if you'd forgotten that story," Anna smiled. "Come on, let's fly off to the water tower."

Her voice sounded once more like the voice Tony knew: strong and eager for adventure! Perhaps a bit too eager for adventure, he thought, suddenly feeling rather uneasy!

Sitting in the Shadows

Soon they reached the little wood where the water tower stood on a slight rise. Bright light shone from the ground-floor windows, and from the open door came the sound of some sort of pop music. In front of the tower stood several little tables with lighted candles. Everything looked calm and inviting, and yet . . . as he thought of Aunt Dorothy and her admirer sitting there, watched by Greg, a shiver ran down Tony's spine.

"Can you see them?" he asked softly.

"Yes!" Anna steered towards a chestnut tree and landed in the top branches. "They're sitting at that table a little apart from the others," she told him in a whisper, as Tony settled next to her. "And there's no candle on their table."

"No candle?" asked Tony, sounding worried. How was he going to recognize Aunt Dorothy? What was more, how was he going to find out whether her admirer really was Mr Crustscrubber's mysterious patient, Igno von Rant?

"I thought you all liked candles?"

"We do," said Anna with dignity. "But when it's overcast, like here, we prefer to stay in the shadows."

"Overcast?" repeated Tony doubtfully. Perhaps she meant overcrowded, but most of the tables were empty, as far as he could see. Presumably all the customers, apart from Aunt Dorothy, her admirer and Greg – and they

80

didn't exactly count as "customers"! – had gone inside. There did seem to be more people inside, though it wasn't exactly overcrowded.

But vampires were wary of people, at least when it came to social gatherings!

"What about Greg?" he asked. "Is he sitting at the table with them?"

"No, he's sitting two tables away," answered Anna.

"In the dark?"

"Yes." Anna paused. "But something isn't quite right . . . "

"Something's not quite right? Do you think he might have . . . seen us?"

"No, he doesn't look like that!" Anna's voice sounded grim.

"What's up then?"

"He's resting his head on the table and, if I'm not mistaken, he's snoring, that lazy good-for-nothing!"

"Snoring?" Tony nearly laughed out loud, in spite of the seriousness of the situation. But if Greg was fast asleep, when he was supposed to be keeping an eye on Aunt Dorothy . . . "It's just like in your fairy-tale," he remarked.

"Oh?" was all Anna said.

"Yes. In the Sleeping Beauty, everyone else was asleep too!"

"Aunt Dorothy isn't asleep," said Anna coolly. She seemed to think Tony was making fun of her fairy-tale. "And Greg's about to wake up," she added. "I'll take care of that!"

"You're going to wake him?" Tony was alarmed. As far as he was concerned, she could let Greg go on sleeping. After all, the Little Vampire himself had on one occasion been afraid to disturb the ever-moody, unpredictable Greg from his sleep!

"What if I do wake him?" said Anna. "After all, Greg promised me faithfully he'd do the job properly. And if he falls asleep, it's *me* who's going to get into trouble!"

"You'll get into trouble?"

"Yes, just like last time when Greg flew away. Afterwards, my grandmother, Sabina the Sinister, got cross with *me*! She said I shouldn't have burdened Greg with such a difficult task."

Anna shook her fists angrily. "He *is* the eldest, but it's always the same old thing: remember that Greg turned into a vampire during his adolescent years, so we must be understanding and patient with the problems he's got now he's a teenager. Huh! I've got absolutely no patience with him if he's neglecting his duty!"

Her mind made up, she spread out her arms under her cloak.

"Come on, Tony! Let's go!"

"I – I'd rather wait here," said Tony.

"Aren't you dying to know more about old Percy Pigeon over there?" asked Anna.

"Who?"

"You know, Aunt Dorothy's admirer! I call him Percy Pigeon because – well, you *must* have heard him billing and cooing at Aunt Dorothy all the time! It's awful!"

Tony hesitated. "What if Aunt Dorothy sees me?"

"I'm sure she won't," answered Anna. "She and her admirer only have eyes for each other."

"They're much, much worse than us two!" she added with a low giggle.

"But what about Greg? Rudolph says Greg always goes completely mad if you disturb him when he's asleep."

"This time he'll be quite peaceful," replied Anna. "After all, he's fallen asleep on the job!"

She spread out her arms under her cloak and glided down to the ground without a sound.

Tony waited a moment longer. When he saw that not one of the vampires seemed to have taken any notice of Anna, he set off after her.

Mean and Underhand

Tony landed behind a thick rose hedge. Only a few steps away was the table at which Greg was sitting – or rather, sleeping. He could hear Greg's snores quite clearly, accompanied by a high, whistling noise.

A little further off he could make out two dark figures, sitting with their heads close together. One was tall and fairly solid, the other smaller and thinner.

"Is that Aunt Dorothy and her admirer?" Tony turned to Anna with a whisper.

"Yes," Anna told him softly.

"Hasn't Aunt Dorothy noticed Greg's asleep?"

"Of course she's noticed," answered Anna. "But it suits her to be with someone who goes to sleep instead of keeping an eye on her."

"And one of these days," Anna went on angrily, "she'll go to the Family Council and complain that *I* switched places with Greg and that Greg just snored the whole time!"

"That's really mean and underhand," said Tony indignantly.

"It is," confirmed Anna. "But her admirer's even more cunning."

"Really?" murmured Tony. He studied the admirer with a feeling of unease. His jet-black hair was brushed back severely and glinted greasily, as though it had been smothered in hair oil.

"He's so cunning that he's even trying to come and settle in with us!" said Anna.

"What, with you?"

"Yes, just imagine – he's asked Aunt Dorothy to marry him."

"No!" gasped Tony.

"He has! If she says yes, he wants to move into the vault!" Anna gave a disgusted snort.

"How do you know all this?" asked Tony.

"How? Because I don't fall asleep when I'm supposed to be keeping an eye on them!"

"And you really heard him asking her to marry him?" Tony still couldn't believe it.

"Not only that," said Anna. "He wants to call himself by her maiden name!"

"Her maiden name?"

"Aunt Dorothy was born a Sackville-Bagg, and since she was widowed, her name has been Sackville-Bagg-Pigsbubble. And Percy Pigeon wants to be a Sackville-Bagg too! He says he's got no spiritual attachment to his own name. Huh!"

"Really?" Tony was trying to keep calm. Here at last was the chance to ask Anna the name of the mysterious admirer. "Is his name that bad then?"

"Bad?" Anna's mouth twisted. "He's so small he's got a name that sounds like Runt!"

"Runt?" Tony's heart was in his mouth.

"Yes, Igno von Rant, actually!" Anna told him laughing bitterly.

Tony watched in horror as the two figures at the table turned their heads and looked in their direction.

A Spy

"There's something in that bush!" Tony heard Aunt Dorothy's voice.

"I expect it's just rabbits," said Igno von Rant.

"Rabbits?" Aunt Dorothy didn't seem convinced.

"Yes, I'm sure that's what it was!" said Igno von Rant with a high-pitched, affected laugh. "Rabbits holding a wedding celebration – just as we will soon, my dear!"

"It wasn't rabbits," retorted Aunt Dorothy. "It's more likely to have been—"

She paused. Tony's heart was beating wildly.

" —to have been that inquisitive nephew of mine!"

"What?" Igno von Rant was beside himself. "Has your family put a spy on us?" He pointed at Greg, who was still snoring. "I've been keeping my fingers crossed that that young rascal would fall asleep, and now are you saying they've sent another one after us?"

"A *niece* this time!" Anna called, and to Tony's dismay she ran round the rose hedge and went up to Aunt Dorothy and Igno von Rant.

"Oh, it's you," said Aunt Dorothy unpleasantly.

"Yes, I wanted to see whether Greg was doing his job properly."

"It's a bit late for that!" said Aunt Dorothy.

"Late?"

"Indeed!" hissed Aunt Dorothy. "A chaperon who snores loudly enough to deafen you is hardly what the

Family Council had in mind!

"And what's more," she went on, "it's highly embarrassing for me and Mr von Rant," she added. "What must he think of our family?"

"I can't help it if Greg's fallen asleep," said Anna defensively.

"But you know the problems he has," retorted Aunt Dorothy. "He's a growing teenage vampire and he's not as tough as others!"

"You always jump to Greg's defence, all of you!" said Anna angrily.

"What had you arranged which was so important that you had to swap with Greg?" Aunt Dorothy inquired, peering suspiciously in Tony's direction.

Tony's heart stood still.

For a second, Anna hesitated. Then she answered calmly "I wanted to look round for a present."

"A present?" Aunt Dorothy laughed scornfully. "What do you need a present for? You're far too spoilt already!"

"It's not for me," replied Anna.

"Not for you?" Once more, Aunt Dorothy looked in Tony's direction. "For whom, then?"

"It's going to be for both of you!" announced Anna merrily.

"Oh, for us . . . "

"Yes, it's a *wedding* present!"

Bad Feelings

Tony could only admire Anna for thinking up such an excuse! Aunt Dorothy's irritable mood was immediately transformed.

"A wedding present!" she repeated, exchanging glances with Igno von Rant.

"Then Anna should be the first to hear the joyful news, don't you think?" she asked.

"Indeed!" Igno von Rant agreed.

"Joyful news?" said Anna, looking as if, like Tony, she was preparing herself for the worst.

"Yes, *very* joyful news! Mr von Rant and I have decided – it's such a clever way of putting it – to embark on a trial marriage. Haven't we, my dear?"

With these words, she stretched out her arm. Igno von Rant grasped it and kissed her affectatiously on the hand. It all looked so funny Tony nearly laughed out loud.

"A trial marriage?" he heard Anna ask.

"Yes, indeed! Most people have a trial marriage nowadays," explained Aunt Dorothy condescendingly. "That way, you can make sure you suit each other in everyday life."

"Every-*day*?" Anna's voice sounded sarcastic.

"That's just a manner of speech," answered Aunt Dorothy. "We're talking about normal, boring, night-to-night goings-on. In any case," she continued, "it will be a big change for dear Mr von Rant. After all, he's been living on his own for a very, very long time. And you three – you and Greg and Rudolph – aren't exactly enthralling company!"

Anna looked over at Greg. "You can say that again!"

"That's why Mr von Rant and I want to see first of all whether we have – " Aunt Dorothy laughed huskily – "whether we have anything left to say to each other under normal circumstances."

"Exactly!" declared Igno von Rant.

"What's more," concluded Aunt Dorothy, "then it won't be necessary to have a chaperone every night."

"Oh, that'd be great!" said Anna with a sigh. After a moment's thought she said, "If it's so difficult for Mr von Rant, why don't *you* move in with *him*, Aunt Dorothy?"

"Don't get involved with things you don't understand!" retorted Aunt Dorothy haughtily.

"But if you moved in with Mr von Rant, you'd both be left in peace – I mean, without Greg, Rudolph and me!" Anna tried again.

"Didn't you hear what I said?" snapped Aunt Dorothy, and this time her voice was sharp. "Keep out of this!"

"I'd love to. I'd have liked to have kept out of the whole thing!"

"Then don't go poking your nose into things that don't concern you!"

"That don't concern me?" said Anna indignantly. "As it happens, I live in the Sackville-Bagg Family Vault as well!"

"More's the pity!" remarked Igno von Rant spitefully.

"Pity?" repeated Anna, not in the least intimidated. "I don't think my brothers would see it like that," she said confidently. "And my mother, Thelma the Thirsty, and father, Frederick the Frightful, certainly wouldn't! And my grandmother, Sabina the Sinister, and grandfather,

89

William the Wild, are both very attached to me as well, because I'm the youngest in the family!"

She paused for breath, before adding, "My family would rather do without *you*!"

"Anna!" cried Aunt Dorothy, sounding shocked, and looking from Igno von Rant to her and back again. "You . . . you must have misunderstood, Anna," she said hastily. "Mr von Rant was only making a joke. Weren't you, dear Igno?" she said. "You were only joking!"

"Joking?" he grumbled unhappily. "I'm not in the habit of joking."

"Sometimes you do," Aunt Dorothy contradicted him. "Tell my little niece" she cooed, "that you didn't mean it like that! Otherwise there'll be bad feelings before my family have even had a chance to get to know you."

"Bad feelings?" repeated Igno von Rant. "In what respect?"

"Well . . . " Aunt Dorothy dropped her voice to a conspiratorial whisper, but Tony could still just hear what she said. "If Anna goes and turns the family against you – against *us* – it would be very difficult. Perhaps my relations might not warm towards you whole-heartedly, and that would be terrible, don't you think?"

"Absolutely," said Igno von Rant, "especially as I've been left out in the cold!"

"Exactly," whispered Aunt Dorothy. "Relations between vampires must be cared for and nurtured! That's why," she added ingratiatingly, "I would love you to be friends – you and my little niece!"

Anyone can Change their Mind

"We've got to be friends, have we?" Igno von Rant studied Anna. "Well, why not? I've got a little idea which might help . . ."

"Oh, really?" answered Anna frostily.

"You're a typical girl, aren't you?" asked Igno von Rant.

"A typical girl?" repeated Anna, highly suspicious.

"Yes! Girls always love dressing up and making themselves look pretty – unlike boys. Isn't that so?"

"Unlike boys?" Anna laughed contemptuously. "No-one likes going round in rags, whether they're boys or girls!"

"Well, all right, whatever you say," Igno von Rant gave in. "But *you* like pretty clothes!"

"Mmm, maybe," said Anna evenly.

"I know you do, because your dear aunt told me," explained Igno von Rant. "And I also know that you've quarrelled about it before now."

"We certainly have!" Anna agreed. "Aunt Dorothy won't let me wear the lace dress I found in the ruins any more!"

"Well," said Aunt Dorothy, "I didn't think it was appropriate. But since I've known Mr von Rant . . . well, anyone can change their mind, can't they?" she concluded.

"You've changed your mind?" Anna still sounded

disbelieving. "Am I really allowed to wear the white lace dress?" she asked after a pause.

"That's not all," declared Igno von Rant boastfully. "The three of us are now going to my house, where I will show you something really pretty!"

"What? Do you want to take Anna back to your house?" said Aunt Dorothy in surprise.

"Why not?" asked Igno von Rant.

"Up till now, you've always insisted we keep your hide-out a secret!" retorted Aunt Dorothy.

"Yes, that's true," said Igno von Rant. "But wasn't it you who said that relations between vampires must be cared for and nurtured? And didn't you also say that you'd like your little niece and I to be friends?"

"Yes, I did," admitted Aunt Dorothy. "But there was no need to invite her to your house straight away!"

"But I can only show her the pretty thing there," explained Igno von Rant. "And our friendship will start with the pretty thing!" he added pompously.

"Is it something . . . to wear?" asked Anna.

"I shan't tell you," answered Igno von Rant. "It will be a surprise!"

With these words, he got up and held out his arm to Aunt Dorothy, just like gentlemen used to do. Aunt Dorothy stood up and hooked her arm through his.

"A surprise?" mumbled Anna.

"Come on, then!" urged Aunt Dorothy. "Don't take advantage of your budding friendship with Mr von Rant by dawdling!"

"I'm coming!" said Anna. She just had time to glance helplessly in Tony's direction, then she set off behind them.

A Friend's Duties

Tony stayed where he was, watching the strange trio: Aunt Dorothy, who was a whole head taller than her admirer, the slight figure of Igno von Rant, and the tiny, dainty Anna. They vanished behind the water tower and Tony breathed again. He had the feeling that his need for adventure had been more than met tonight. On the other hand, he remembered how desperate Mr Crustscrubber had been to know more about his unusual patient – he didn't even have his address . . .

This was just the opportunity Tony was waiting for, to find out where Igno von Rant's hide-out lay, where he was taking Anna . . . His heart beat faster at the thought of Anna. Hadn't she hesitated at Igno von Rant's suggestion to go to his house? What if danger threatened, not from Aunt Dorothy, but from Igno von Rant?

After all, it hadn't yet been proved beyond doubt that Igno von Rant really *was* a vampire. And only if he were one could Anna be sure that he didn't have something evil in store for her!

Wasn't it his duty, as a friend, to stand by Anna? Tony didn't feel he could rely on Aunt Dorothy to help her. After all, Aunt Dorothy had set off without paying the slightest attention to the helpless, sleeping Greg. Tony looked over at Greg, whose head lay in the same place on the table, snoring loudly and regularly.

The vampires had simply abandoned him! It showed once more just how strict the rule was governing their lives: "Think of yourself, first and every time!" Only Anna wasn't like that; at least, not all the time. She put herself out for other people, just as he, Tony, did. *He* took care of his friends, especially his vampire friends. He would never have left Greg lying there so helpless.

Tony bent down and searched the ground for some object he could use to wake Greg up. He found a conker. He quickly stood up again, took aim and threw it.

The last thing he saw was Greg's head with its shaggy mop of hair bobbing up in the air, still half-asleep.

Then he raced away. He ran without stopping till he reached a light. Then he spread out his arms, moved them up and down a couple of times, and flew.

As Tony climbed into the air, he searched around desperately for Aunt Dorothy, Igno von Rant and Anna. But there was no one to be seen. Could they have flown so quickly that they had already reached Igno von Rant's hide-out?

But they had only left about five minutes ago, and Aunt Dorothy's heavy build didn't make for a speedy flyer!

Which direction should Tony go? He didn't even know his way back home from here!

He made uncertainly for a street bordered by tall trees, and almost cried out loud with relief: down below, he caught sight of the vampire trio, marching along the pavement. Igno von Rant was in front, with Aunt Dorothy on his arm and Anna behind them, very small and sweet in her long black cloak.

Tony slowed his flight and landed behind one of the trees. He looked over anxiously at the dark figures. But the three continued on their way without hesitating. He waited for a moment, then started to follow them, keeping in the shadows of the trees.

He had never been in this particular street before. Everything looked unfamiliar and rather strange: there were so few parked cars, the road was full of potholes, and in many of the gardens the grass was standing knee-high.

It was just like in a ghost town! The thought shot through his mind. But no, in a ghost town there wouldn't be a child's bicycle leaning against a garden fence, nor a skipping rope left lying on the pavement.

What was more, lights were shining from several houses, so there were people living here after all.

People . . . Tony studied the group of vampires and a shudder ran down his spine. He would have preferred a less deserted neighbourhood, just in case of an emergency!

But no human being crossed their path.

Clear View Villa

When they reached the last street lamp in the road, Igno von Rant, Aunt Dorothy and Anna suddenly stopped. Igno von Rant went over and opened a garden gate which made a low, rattling noise. Aunt Dorothy looked round suspiciously at the sound, but just in time, Tony ducked away behind a large tree.

Cautiously he peered round the trunk.

Igno von Rant, Aunt Dorothy and Anna went up to a large, dark house. Seconds later, they had vanished.

Did Igno von Rant have his hideout somewhere in that house? Tony couldn't believe it! Cemeteries, vaults, chapels, ruins . . . all these were very suitable for vampires. But a house, a normal house . . . ?

However, the house was not so normal after all, Tony realized almost at once. As he drew nearer, he could see that it must have been standing empty for a long time as the door and ground-floor windows had been boarded up. It didn't look very inviting: its walls were black with age, and its chimney falling down.

Even if Tony wasn't in a ghost *town*, this was definitely a ghost *house* – the ideal hideout for someone who wanted to remain undiscovered!

Tony wondered whether it would be better to sneak up to the house from the garden next door. But presumably the vampires had gone into the cellar, so it didn't really matter which side he approached the house from, as long as he was quiet enough.

When he reached the garden gate, he paused and decided not to open it in case the rattling noise reached the vampires' ears and warned them!

Very carefully, he climbed over the fence, which had sharp iron spikes that stuck up dangerously. Then he slipped through the long grass up to the front door.

Tony peered anxiously at the houses on either side. But nothing stirred. Possibly the next-door houses were empty as well, he thought. He turned back to the door, which was boarded over with planks. If Igno von Rant had moved in here, *this* house wasn't exactly empty!

Just then, Tony noticed a sign on the wall. With some difficulty he managed to decipher what was written, by the light of the street lamps:

> If pure of heart and clear of view,
> Take a chance – fortune beckons you!
> *Clear View Villa*

He couldn't help but grin. The verse was presumably some sort of blessing for the house, but it was true in only one sense: "pure of heart". That expression was just made for a vampire's lair!

But Villa? "Dingy Den" would have been more appropriate! And "clear of view" through boarded-up windows? No, "take a chance" could only mean one thing in Clear View Villa, as far as he was concerned: take your chance, and leave! Fortune seemed to have deserted this house a long time ago.

Voices from Below

At that moment, the little mound of stones and rubble on which Tony was perched gave way under his feet with a rattling crunch.

It gave him a shock. He took a step to one side. I hope the vampires didn't catch any of that, he thought, as his eyes wandered over the faded façade of the house.

If Aunt Dorothy, Igno von Rant and Anna were in the cellars, as Tony presumed, the danger was not so pressing. But if, on the other hand, they had gone up to the first floor . . . Up there, there were no boards nailed across the windows, and their empty sockets stared back at Tony black and sinister. But surely a vampire would never set up home under such a dilapidated roof, Tony suddenly thought. It would let in the sunshine and rain!

Suddenly he heard distant voices: one deep and rasping, the other bright and slightly husky. They sounded strangely muffled, as though they were coming up from below ground.

So the vampires really had gone down to the cellar! But – where was the entrance? They couldn't have entered Clear View Villa through the front door: the boards were far too firmly fixed for that. Perhaps there were cellar steps leading down from the back of the house?

Walking on tiptoe, Tony left the front entrance and found a path, overgrown with grass, which led round the house to the left. He took a couple of careful steps, then stopped still and listened. Now he could hear the voices again. They still sounded oddly muffled, but they were so close that he could pick up every word.

"So you really don't want to look at the pretty thing?" asked Igno von Rant.

"Yes, I do!" said Anna. "But only if you'll come with me, Mr von Rant. I'm not going up there on my own."

Up there? Tony pressed himself more closely against the wall of the house. He could only pray that the "pretty thing" was on the ground floor with its boarded windows, and not on the first floor!

"Why do you call him Mr von Rant?" piped Aunt Dorothy. "Why not call him Uncle Igno?"

"Yes, why not?" agreed Igno von Rant.

"Why should I?" retorted Anna.

"To bring us vampires closer together," answered Aunt Dorothy.

"Hmm, I'll think about it," said Anna, but it was easy to tell that she wasn't very keen on the idea.

"Then let's do something about getting closer together!" remarked Igno von Rant, ignoring Anna's barely concealed hostility. And in an oily tone he added, "So dear little Anna doesn't dare go on her own! How sweet! That's really sweet!"

Tony clenched his fists. Igno von Rant was the last person he'd allow to call Anna "sweet".

"Don't I dare?" repeated Anna. "What do you mean, Mr von Rant?"

"Well, you've always been a bit of a coward," Aunt Dorothy put in.

Tony felt the blood rush to his face with anger at this wicked suggestion.

"I'm supposed to be cowardly, am I?" Anna gave an

100

angry little laugh. "All right then, if I'm such a coward, I shall tell the Family Council that you've been telling family secrets to Mr von Rant!"

"What? You'll tell the Family Council?" Aunt Dorothy was aghast. "No, you mustn't do that, Anna! For Dracula's sake, don't say anything horrible about me and Mr von Rant to the Family Council!"

"Then *you* must take back what you said about me being a coward!" Anna demanded.

"Of course I'll take it back," murmured Aunt Dorothy. "You're actually quite brave!"

She certainly is! Tony agreed, but only to himself.

Night Blindness

"If your little niece is so brave, why won't she go upstairs on her own?" Igno von Rant declared.

"Why?" said Anna. "Because *you* know your way round here much better than I do, Mr von Rant, and because *I* don't want to bump my head or stub my toe!"

"But isn't it true that you all have eyes as sharp as an owl's?" asked Igno von Rant.

"All of us?" asked Anna. "Who are you talking about?"

"You – your family," answered Igno von Rant, clearing his throat. "You Sackville-Baggs are renowned for your sharp eyes!"

"Our eyes are quite normal," said Anna, "like any other vampire's."

"Not *any* other vampire's!" Aunt Dorothy corrected her. "Mr von Rant unfortunately doesn't have such good eyes."

"What's wrong with his eyes?" Anna asked.

"Well . . . he suffers a little from night blindness, poor Mr von Rant."

"Night blindness?" Anna repeated.

"Yes," Aunt Dorothy gave a little cough. Obviously Igno von Rant's poor sight was a painful matter for her. "It can happen in the best vampire circles."

"Oh, really?" said Anna. "*I've* never heard of a vampire with night blindness."

Then she added pointedly, "The main thing is, I hope this night blindness isn't catching!"

"Anna, don't say such a thing!" implored Aunt Dorothy. "And above all, not a word about it to the Family Council!"

"Why not?"

"Because . . . " Aunt Dorothy paused. Then she explained solemnly, "Because you should always judge your fellow creatures by what they *are*, and not by what they are *not*! And if it were known at the Family Council that Mr von Rant had a few – problems with his eyes, then they might all take against him. And anyway," she concluded, "that's just the reason why I respect dear Mr von Rant!"

"What? Because he can't see properly?" exclaimed Anna.

"No. Because he's not just like everybody else," replied Aunt Dorothy with dignity, adding softly, "You can turn on your torch, dearest Igno. Anna will understand. And Anna doesn't hold anything against you for it, do you?"

"No," said Anna. What else could she say?

"Switch on the torch?" Igno von Rant gave an embarrassed laugh. "If you say so, Dorothy dear."

He must have been holding the torch already, for at once Tony saw a beam of light coming from a low-lying cellar window. Like the ground floor windows, it was boarded over with planks, but rather more haphazardly. Several of the planks were missing, so that even Aunt Dorothy could have squeezed through.

Tony's heart beat faster at the thought. Perhaps the vampires hadn't got into the house via the cellar steps after all, but through this very window!

The beam of light quivered and grew weaker. Then

Tony heard Igno von Rant's voice. "Follow me, Anna! Then you'll see the pretty thing in just a moment. What am I talking about, see it? You'll be wearing it! Just wait a moment. I know you'll love it!"

"Yes, you two go on ahead," said Aunt Dorothy. "I'm going to have a quick look outside, just to be on the safe side."

A quick look outside? For a second, Tony was rooted to the spot with horror. But then, as something began to move behind the boards, he raced away.

As fast as he could, he ran to the gate and climbed over it. Out on the pavement, he turned round and looked back at the house. There it stood, dismal and forbidding, without the slightest sign of life.

Tony felt guilty as he thought of Anna. Had he left her in the lurch by running away from Aunt Dorothy? But Anna hadn't sounded in the slightest bit intimidated or worried. No, she'd know how to look after herself, if it came to that! Tony spread out his arms under the cloak, moved them up and down a couple of times, and rose up into the air.

Sleeping in your Shoes

It was a long and tiring flight home. Tony had to fly back to the water tower, and from there almost the whole way to Mr Crustscrubber's, before he finally recognized a street he knew would lead him back home.

Exhausted, he reached his room at last and dropped on to his bed with a deep sigh. He just wanted to rest for a moment . . .

"Have you fallen asleep in your shoes?" a bright voice suddenly said close by.

"Me?" Tony shot upright, uncertain whether he was awake or dreaming. In a beam of silvery moonlight stood a small figure – like an apparition from the spirit world. He rubbed his eyes in bewilderment.

Now the figure gave a giggle, and all at once, Tony knew who it was.

"Anna!" he said.

"You look really lovable when you're asleep, Tony!" She gave another giggle.

"When I'm asleep?" He scratched his head with embarrassment. "I . . . I was just going to lie down for a minute."

"You were smiling," said Anna softly. "You were probably dreaming about us!"

"Or about taking my shoes off!" retorted Tony, to turn the conversation in a different direction. He stretched out his legs on the bed and began to untie the laces.

"You must quite like wearing shoes," said Anna. "In fact, I think it's really good that you're practising!"

Tony lifted his head. "Practising? Do you think I don't know how to take off my shoes by myself?"

"No, of course not!" She laughed huskily. "I meant, you haven't had as much practice as *we* have in sleeping with your shoes on – not yet, anyway!" she added.

Now Tony understood what she was getting at!

"I don't want to practise sleeping with my shoes on!" he declared, turning back to his left shoelace, which had got itself into a tight knot.

Anna didn't answer. Had Tony's words made her angry? Without looking up he asked, "Is your dress the 'pretty thing' Igno von Rant wanted to show you?"

"Huh! It doesn't matter, does it?" snapped Anna. "You obviously don't like it!"

"What makes you think that?"

"Firstly, when you woke up just now, you didn't say one word about my dress. And secondly, you haven't looked at me once!"

"That's because I want to take off my shoes," Tony defended himself. He finally succeeded in undoing the knot. With a sigh, he pulled off the shoe. "And what's more, I can't see much anyway with the light off."

"Can't you see anything?" Anna went over to the desk and switched on the lamp. "Is that better?"

"Yes." The sudden bright light dazzled Tony for a moment. When his eyes had got used to it, he studied Anna. She was wearing a long dress made of a pink material which had the sheen of silk. It fitted her extremely well, almost as though it had been made for her. It was probably an old dress that had once belonged to a child.

"Well?" asked Anna, with badly concealed curiosity.

"You – you look very smart!" said Tony cautiously. He didn't want to put his foot in it again!

"Smart?" Anna smiled and looked pleased, running her hands down the dress. "Really?"

"Yes. Smart and — " Tony hesitated.

Anna frowned. "And what?"

If Tony wanted to be truthful – really truthful – he should have said that she looked like a doll, not the Anna he knew and liked so much. But sometimes telling the truth can be hurtful and unkind, and so he simply said, "Smart and – different!"

"Different?" repeated Anna, and to Tony's relief she smiled. "Yes, that's true! If you compare this fantastic dress with the old rags I usually wear . . . Mr von Rant's got other pretty things too," she told him.

"Has he?" said Tony, trying hard not to let Anna see how keen he was to hear more about Igno von Rant.

"He certainly has!" Anna gathered up her dress and came to sit next to Tony. "He's got an enormous cupboard, and he's the only person with a key to it!"

"On the ground floor?" asked Tony excitedly.

Anna looked at him in surprise. "Do you know about the cupboard?"

"No, I don't know about the cupboard."

"But you just asked about the ground floor."

"Yes, because . . . I followed you to the house." Tony cleared his throat. Anna wouldn't be cross that he had followed them, would she?

"You followed us?"

"Yes. I was worried. I didn't want to leave you alone with that Igno von Rant!"

Now Anna giggled. "I wouldn't say you were worried," she said. "More like . . . " She gave a meaningful pause and looked tenderly at Tony.

"More like what?"

"I'd say you were *jealous*," replied Anna. "Jealous because you're in love!"

Something to get Excited About

Tony felt himself blush. "Jealous?" he said innocently. "Jealous of whom?"

"You may well ask!" giggled Anna. "But don't worry, I'm not going to keep Uncle Igno's presents!"

"*Uncle* Igno?" asked Tony irritably. "I thought you didn't want to call him 'Uncle'!"

"I didn't," said Anna easily. "But anyone can change their mind!"

"Just like Aunt Dorothy!" remarked Tony spitefully.

"Yes, isn't that amazing?" Anna laughed. "Aunt Dorothy said I could wear the dress as often as I like!"

"As often as you like?" repeated Tony. That was really something to get excited about . . .

After a pause, he asked, "You said *presents*. What else was there?"

Without a word, but with a mysterious smile, Anna pulled a long golden chain from the neck of her dress. On it hung a little heart, set with blue and green stones.

"He gave you a gold necklace?" Tony was growing more and more suspicious.

"He lent it to me!" said Anna with dignity. "I told you, I'm not accepting his presents!"

"Lent it? I thought vampires didn't know the difference between lending and giving!"

"You must have read that in one of your vampire books!" said Anna, giggling.

"No, Rudolph told me, on your Vampire Day."

"Rudolph? Well, now you know what fibs he tells. But I weakened when it came to Uncle Igno's rings!" she added, holding out her right hand to Tony. Gold rings twinkled on her middle finger and index finger. One was set with a blood-red stone, the other with a whitish one.

"Are they real jewels?" asked Tony.

"Of course!" said Anna proudly. "The red one's a ruby, Uncle Igno said, and the white one's a moonstone." She ran her fingertips thoughtfully over the white stone.

"Don't you think that's a beautiful name, moonstone?" she asked.

"I — " Tony cleared his throat. Even though Anna was in such raptures about it all, it still seemed very suspicious to Tony that Igno von Rant had given her the dress and the jewellery.

"It all looks like a bribe to me," he said.

"A bribe?" Anna giggled. "Oh, Tony, you're even more jealous than Rudolph was about Olga! I think it's touching – really touching!"

"Touching?" said Tony, looking grim.

Anna giggled again. "I'd have thought you wouldn't have any objection to my new uncle lending me a few pretty things. But if you're as jealous as all that . . . Anyway, I only made myself look pretty for you," she added tenderly, "so you would see I'm not the Cinderella Rudolph always says I am!"

"I never said you were a Cinderella!" retorted Tony. He was starting to get the same feeling he had when he talked to Rudolph about Olga – as if he was speaking to a brick wall. Whatever Tony said, Anna would just giggle happily and say he had something against Uncle Igno.

But there was one thing he had to discuss with her

111

urgently: something that might be of the greatest importance to the Little Vampire, and perhaps to Anna too!

Jealousy

"About Igno von Rant's eyes — " he began. "Didn't Aunt Dorothy say he suffered from night blindness?"

"Just a little, she said," Anna corrected him.

"All right, he suffers a little from night blindness," said Tony. "But he can't see much in the dark, can he?"

"He found the keyhole in the cupboard first go!"

"Yes, because he had the torch with him."

"But he took the torch with him mainly for my sake," Anna said.

"For your sake?" said Tony doubtfully.

"Oh, Tony!" She laughed softly. "You really are too sweet with all this jealousy! He switched on the torch so that I could choose the prettiest out of all the dresses – there were at least twenty. And of course, that was easier with some light than without." Tony's feeling that he was talking to a brick wall grew even stronger. However, he made a last attempt.

"Do you know how long Igno von Rant has had this problem with his eyes?"

"No, no idea," replied Anna, adding with a giggle, "Even if you won't believe me, I tell you I really don't care a fig for Uncle Igno."

Tony sighed. "That's not what this is all about!"

"Oh?" Anna gave him a coquettish smile. "What is it about then?"

"About you!"

"I know that!" she said softly. "That's why I'm not angry that you're so jealous – quite the contrary, in fact."

"It's about your *eyes*!" Tony made a final attempt.

"My eyes?" Anna blinked a couple of times. "Now I suppose you're going to say I've been gazing too deeply into Uncle Igno's eyes!"

"No!" cried Tony. He pressed his lips together. He'd never known Anna so unapproachable before.

"Do you remember Mr Crustscrubber's lighting equipment?" he asked.

"You bet I do!" said Anna. "Did you think I'd forget such an unfair thing: that Rudolph had some sunglasses and I didn't!"

"Perhaps Igno von Rant didn't have sunglasses either!" remarked Tony.

"What do you mean?"

Tony took a deep breath. At long last Anna seemed prepared to listen to what he had to say!

"Do you remember the mysterious patient I told you about, the one Mr Crustscrubber had already started his treatment on?" he said, looking at her inquiringly.

"Yes, well?"

"This patient, who Mr Crustscrubber says isn't a vampire – is Igno von Rant!"

"Igno von Rant?" repeated Anna in bewilderment. Then the corners of her mouth began to twitch and she said with a giggle, "Tony! You're so jealous you're seeing spooks! Do you really believe that? Uncle Igno seeing Mr Crustscrubber – that's just too ridiculous!"

"What if I tell you that I've met him twice at Mr Crustscrubber's house?"

"*In* his house?" Anna did not seem in the least bit worried, more amused. "It must have been his double! Or else you really are seeing ghosts!"

"What about this evening at the water tower?" replied Tony. "Was that a ghost sitting at the table with Greg and Aunt Dorothy?"

"No!" giggled Anna. "But it was rather dark by the water tower," she said after a pause. "At least, for human eyes."

"Exactly so!" said Tony. "I recognized him from his voice, his figure and his greasy hair. It was just his lily of the valley perfume that was missing, but I suppose he keeps that for his visits to Mr Crustscrubber!"

"Lily of the valley perfume?" asked Anna, no longer sounding quite so carefree. "What does lily of the valley smell like?"

"Sweet, terribly sweet, like — " Tony thought quickly of something suitable to compare the scent with. "I can't describe it," he said.

"Smell it for yourself then," Anna agreed, and to Tony's amazement, she pulled a little round bottle out of the pocket of her dress.

She took out the stopper and held the bottle out to Tony.

"Here. Uncle Igno gave me this bottle for special occasions. Is that lily of the valley perfume?"

Tony coughed. "Yes, it is," he said croakily. "That's the scent he wears: the most powerful sort of lily of the valley. Yuk!"

"So it's true, he *is* the patient," Anna admitted slowly. "Hmm, well, there's nothing wrong with Uncle Igno taking sessions with Mr Crustscrubber," she added after thinking it over for a while.

"He's had several," Tony corrected her. "But now he hasn't been for a couple of weeks. Mr Crustscrubber told me, and he's very worried about it."

"Worried?"

115

"Yes, and so am I."

"Why you?" Anna laughed brightly. "Why should you be worried about Uncle Igno?"

"I'm not worried about *him!*" replied Tony. "About you – and Rudolph!"

"Rudolph?" said Anna, looking sulky. Tony took another deep breath. On no account did he want to upset Anna, or to strengthen her belief that he was jealous of Igno von Rant.

"It's to do with Igno von Rant's night blindness," he began carefully. "Something occurred to me."

"What?"

"The lighting equipment! Perhaps the glaring light from it has harmed his eyes!"

"You think it's because he looked at the light that he's become night blind?" asked Anna, sounding unconvinced.

"Well — " said Tony. "At the moment it's only a hunch. But if I'm right, then you and Rudolph are in danger too."

"Yes . . . " said Anna. She still didn't seem to be taking Tony's warning particularly seriously.

Three Times Thirteen

"But I can easily find that out," she said, sliding off Tony's bed, "now Uncle Igno and I are getting on so well together!"

Lifting the hem of her dress, she went over to the window. There she stood still and said, "Now you must turn round, Tony."

"Turn round? Why?"

"So that you'll remember me in this lovely dress, and not in my shabby old vampire cloak."

"Remember you?" said Tony, puzzled. "Aren't we going to see each other again?"

"Of course we are," said Anna with a soft laugh. "But if you remember what I looked like in this dress, perhaps you'll dream of me tonight. And perhaps you'll dream that we're together forever."

Tony blushed and quickly turned his head towards the wall.

"No, I don't think so," he said. "I only ever dream about school."

"I don't believe it!" said Anna with a giggle.

Tony heard the silk material rustle mysteriously. Presumably Anna had just pulled the vampire cloak around her. "That white lace dress from the ruins . . ." he began, with his eyes fixed on the rough surface of the wallpaper. "Wouldn't you like to take it with you? I mean, now Aunt Dorothy's changed her mind?"

"No, I'd rather not," she answered. "First I must wait and see whether it's going to be a permanent change of mind. Anyway, I'd like it if something of mine stays here with you, even if it is only a dress!" she added. "And now, goodnight, Tony. Promise me you'll count to thirteen three times before you turn round."

Tony grinned. "Three times to thirteen? I don't know if I can manage that . . . "

"Shall I help you?" she teased. "With three times thirteen kisses?"

"No, thank you, that won't be necessary," he said. "I think if I concentrate, I should be able to do it!"

"Then – see you soon, Tony!"

"Yes, see you!" he replied. And in a monotonous voice he began to count: "One, two, three . . . "

Tony had got to twelve when he heard keys jingling in the hallway outside and father's familiar words, "There, you see, Hilary? All's quiet."

Tony whipped round. Hastily, he pulled the vampire cloak over his head and hid it under his bed. Then he ran to his desk and switched off the light. As he did so, he stumbled against the chair which fell over with a loud crash.

Tony waited. It sounded like an explosion in the silence of the house . . .

As he groped his way back to bed, he could hear his mother's anxious voice: "That came from Tony's room!"

There was a knocking on the door.

"Tony?" she asked.

He didn't answer.

Now she was rattling at the locked door. "Tony, get up! We know you're awake."

"What is it . . . " he asked, trying to sound as sleepy as possible.

"What was that noise just now in your room?"

"Oh, that . . . " Tony yawned loudly. "I fell out of bed."

"You fell out of bed?" she repeated.

"Yes, and it's time you fell into yours, your wedding party's gone on so late!" he said.

"Cheeky!" she hissed.

Tony heard her steps moving away.

He grinned happily, pulled the bedclothes up to his chin and fell asleep.

Spots

When Tony looked in the bathroom mirror on Monday morning, the face that stared back at him had dark rings under its eyes and a yellow complexion.

No, it wasn't just yellow. He peered closer at the mirror in disbelief. He had funny little red marks round his mouth – dozens of little red spots, each no bigger than a pinhead. Could they be midge bites? No, there were too many of them and they were close together. It must be a rash! thought Tony. He must have eaten something that didn't agree with him. Ollie got a rash if he ate strawberries, but Tony hadn't eaten any strawberries yesterday . . .

Nervously, he bit his lip. Suppose the spots had something to do with Anna? She had come very close to him on Saturday evening, on Mr Crustscrubber's windowsill – she had said she could never be *too* close to him . . .

And later on, Anna had been in his room and shown him her new pink dress.

Then suddenly he remembered! Henry had missed school for a week . . . because he had chicken pox!

An icy feeling ran through Tony. That would be the most dreadful catastrophe! This afternoon he had planned to cycle round the area near the water tower till he found Clear View Villa. He was sure he'd be able to recognize the large, dismal house easily. But if he had

chicken pox, then all his lovely plans were up the creek. No, it just couldn't happen. He *had* to ride his bike over there this afternoon!

"Tony?" He could hear his mother's voice as she came out of the kitchen. "Why are you taking so long?"

"Just coming!"

He turned on the tap and held his face in the stream of cold water. Then he rubbed the skin round his mouth with a flannel. A glance in the mirror convinced him that the little spots were no longer noticeable against his flushed, red skin. Even so, he brushed his teeth and combed his hair carefully, so as to make the best possible impression at breakfast.

That Strange Boy Again

Unfortunately, his efforts were wasted. No sooner had Tony sat down at the table than his father began to laugh.

"Hey, Tony, have you been trying out my razor?"

"What do you mean?" Tony retorted. Trying to keep calm, he began to butter his toast.

"Well, your chin looks so red!" Tony's father laughed again.

"That's the cold water," explained Tony.

"You washed in *cold* water?" His mother's mouth twitched scornfully. "That's a new one!"

"Yeah – I saw it on telly. Cold water keeps the skin looking young for longer. You ought to try it some time."

"Oh, should I?" she said pointedly. "Did they show you a cure for chicken pox on the telly as well?"

Tony went pale. "Chicken pox?"

She nodded. "If I'm not mistaken, those red marks round your mouth are chicken pox."

Tony's slice of toast and honey almost fell from his hand.

"How could I have caught that?" he said in surprise.

"From school, I expect!" She stood up. "I'll give your school office a call. Perhaps they'll know if anyone else has it."

"There's no need," Tony answered hastily. "I, er . . . " He coughed with embarrassment. "Henry's got it."

She sat down again. "Why didn't you say so in the first place?" she asked, looking at Tony searchingly.

"Because — " he hesitated. It wasn't easy to think up an excuse that she would believe.

"I expect Tony had something important planned that he didn't want to miss," remarked Dad. "A date with a girl, perhaps . . . "

"That's right!" said Tony, thankful for his help.

His mother didn't look convinced. "Tony – and a girl?"

"No, not a girl. But it's true I wanted to meet someone: Geoff."

That was actually partly true. Tony had planned to go to Mr Crustscrubber's and tell him about the villa.

"Geoff?" Mum shook her head energetically. "Not that strange boy we haven't met again!"

"Strange boy?" Tony grinned to himself.

"And because of this mysterious Geoff, you want to go to school with chicken pox?" his mother demanded.

"Well — " Tony cleared his throat. "It might not be chicken pox at all. Anyway, we've got to practise for the tournament."

"What tournament?" she asked suspiciously.

"There's a table-tennis tournament in school next Wednesday."

Tony's father nodded approvingly. "Our son's gradually turning into a proper sports' fan!"

"Tony won't be competing in this tournament!" Tony's mother snapped.

"Why not?" Tony was indignant.

"Because chicken pox is very infectious," she replied calmly. "As far as I'm aware, children with chicken pox have to be kept in quarantine."

"In quarantine?"

"Yes. They can't go to school for a week."

"What, a whole week?" exclaimed Tony.

"Sometimes even longer," she replied. "But first of all we must take your temperature. Go back to your room and I'll be with you right away."

If there was one thing Tony hated more than Mondays, it was having his temperature taken. But he did as he was told, and went off to his room.

"In quarantine . . . " he fumed, when he was back in bed. His mother would be bound to say he couldn't leave the flat all week in case he infected the neighbours' children. But there was still a slight chance that it might turn out to be some sort of rash after all!

In Quarantine

Tony's mother took the thermometer out of his mouth. "38.6°," she announced. "That means you've got a temperature."

"A temperature?" murmured Tony. "So is it chicken pox after all?"

"I'm not a doctor," she replied. "But everything points to it."

"Here's something about temperatures!" Tony's father butted in. He had fetched the big encyclopaedia of health from the bookshelf and now began to read out loud: "Usually chicken pox is accompanied by a slight temperature of up to 38°. In severe cases, the temperature may rise to 39° or 40°."

"Severe cases?" Tony gulped.

"What complications can crop up with chicken pox?" continued Dad. "Firstly, the spots can become infected. Secondly, in rare cases, a lung infection may occur. Thirdly, occasionally chicken pox is followed by a—"

Before he could read any further, Mum interrupted. "You'll make Tony nervous!" Turning to her son, she said, "Don't worry, chicken pox is quite a harmless childhood illness."

"Harmless?" grumbled Tony. "I can't go out for a whole week and I've been practising for our table tennis tournament all for nothing, and you think that's harmless?"

Tony's mother didn't let herself get annoyed.

"I'm going to phone Dr Dozee and then we'll see," was all she said.

Tony glanced at his television set, which had been broken for what seemed like an eternity.

"*See?*" he said with a dry laugh. "It'd be nice if we *could* see!"

"Dad and I are glad you aren't constantly watching that thing," replied his mother.

"Glad?" Tony felt his eyes fill with tears. "I only watch telly all the time because of all the bad luck I have!"

"Your date must have been incredibly important after all!" Dad joked. "Just as I said, I bet it's all to do with a girl! Not a Geoff, but a Julia!"

Refusing to rise to the bait, Tony simply pulled the bedclothes over his head.

"Let's go," he heard his mother say. "What Tony needs above all is rest."

The door clicked, and his parents' footsteps faded away. Rest? thought Tony, sticking his head back out from the covers. That was one thing he was going to get more than enough of during the next few days!

Find out what happens to Tony and his vampire friends in the next book in this series, *The Little Vampire Gets a Surprise*.

THE LITTLE VAMPIRE series

Watch out for new titles in the spooky Little Vampire series:

Book 1: **The Little Vampire in Danger**

Book 2: **The Little Vampire in the Vale of Doom**

Book 3: **The Little Vampire in Despair**

Book 4: **The Little Vampire and the Mystery Patient**

Book 5: **The Little Vampire in the Lion's Den**

Book 6: **The Little Vampire Learns to be Brave**

Book 7: **The Little Vampire Gets a Surprise**

Book 8: **The Little Vampire and the Wicked Plot**

These books can be bought or ordered at your local bookshop. For more information about these and other good books, contact *The Sales Department, Simon & Schuster Young Books, Campus 400, Maylands Avenue, Hemel Hempstead HP2 7EZ.*

THE PEEPING DUCK GANG

Follow the hilarious adventures of Howard, Nina and Bob the cowardly dog in this funny detective series:

Book 1: **The Case of the Phantom of the Opera**

Book 2: **The Case of the Missing Teeth**

Book 3: **The Case of the Dream Stealer**

Book 4: **The Case of the Yeti's Footprint**

Book 5: **The Case of the Revenge of the Killer Budgies**

These books can be bought from your local bookstore. If you would like to find out more about these and other good books, write to: *The Sales Department, Simon & Schuster Young Books, Campus 400, Maylands Avenue, Hemel Hempstead HP2 7EZ.*

DRINA

Follow Drina's fortunes, from her first ballet lessons to her triumphant appearances on stages throughout the world, in the gripping Drina series:

You can buy any of these books at your local bookshop. For more information about these and other good books, write to: *The Sales Department, Simon & Schuster Young Books, Campus 400, Maylands Avenue, Hemel Hempstead HP2 7EZ.*